LITTLE,
BROWN

L B

LARGE
PRINT

WITCH & WIZARD

THE GIFT

JAMES PATTERSON

and Ned Rust

LITTLE, BROWN AND COMPANY

LARGE PRINT EDITION

Little, Brown and Company

Hachette Book Group
237 Park Avenue, New York, NY 10017
Visit our website at www.lb-teens.com

Little, Brown and Company is a division of Hachette Book Group, Inc. The Little, Brown name and logo are trademarks of Hachette Book Group, Inc.

First Edition: December 2010
First International Edition: November 2010

The characters and events in this book are fictitious. Any similarity to real persons, living or dead, is coincidental and not intended by the author.

Witch & Wizard: The Gift features excerpts from the following public-domain works: "Lines, On Hearing That Lady Byron Was Ill" by Lord Byron, page 74; "The Road Not Taken" by Robert Frost, pages 169–70; "The Tyger" by William Blake, pages 172–73; "The Conqueror Worm" by Edgar Allan Poe, page 211; "The Fish" by William Butler Yeats, pages 286–87; "Youth and Age" by Samuel Taylor Coleridge, page 312; "The Raven" by Edgar Allan Poe, page 363.

Library of Congress Cataloging-in-Publication Data
Patterson, James.
     The gift / James Patterson & Ned Rust. — 1st ed.
        p. cm. — (Witch & wizard)
     Summary: After escaping imprisonment by the totalitarian regime known as the New Order, siblings Wisty and Whit Allgood, who possess magical powers, establish themselves as leaders of the Resistance, a hidden community of teenagers like themselves, hunted by the state and determined to defy its ban on the arts, magic, and all other forms of creativity.
     ISBN 978-0-316-03625-2 / LP ISBN 978-0-316-12198-9 / International edition ISBN 978-0-316-09872-4
     [1. Brothers and sisters—Fiction.   2. Magic—Fiction.
3. Totalitarianism—Fiction.]   I. Rust, Ned.   II. Title.
     PZ7.P27653Gi 2010
     [Fic] —dc22   2010010706

10   9   8   7   6   5   4   3   2   1

RRD-C

Printed in the United States of America

For Jack, who got me started,
after I got him started.
—J.P.

For Ruth, for laughing at the right times.
—N.R.

NOTICE OF PUBLIC EXECUTION

ATTENTION ALL CITIZENS:

WISTERIA ROSE ALLGOOD, leader and last hope of the pernicious "Resistance" that has destroyed our peace of mind and diverted so much of our citizenry's efforts and resources, has been apprehended and will be **PUBLICLY EXECUTED** in the **COURTYARD OF JUSTICE** at **ONE O'CLOCK** this afternoon. Still wanted for collusion, conspiracy, and experimentation with the dark and foul arts is her brother, **WHITFORD P. ALLGOOD**.

So decreed by The One Who Is The One, this two hundred thirty-fifth day of the first year of the New Order's Ascendancy.

BOOK ONE

THE GIRL WITH THE GIFT

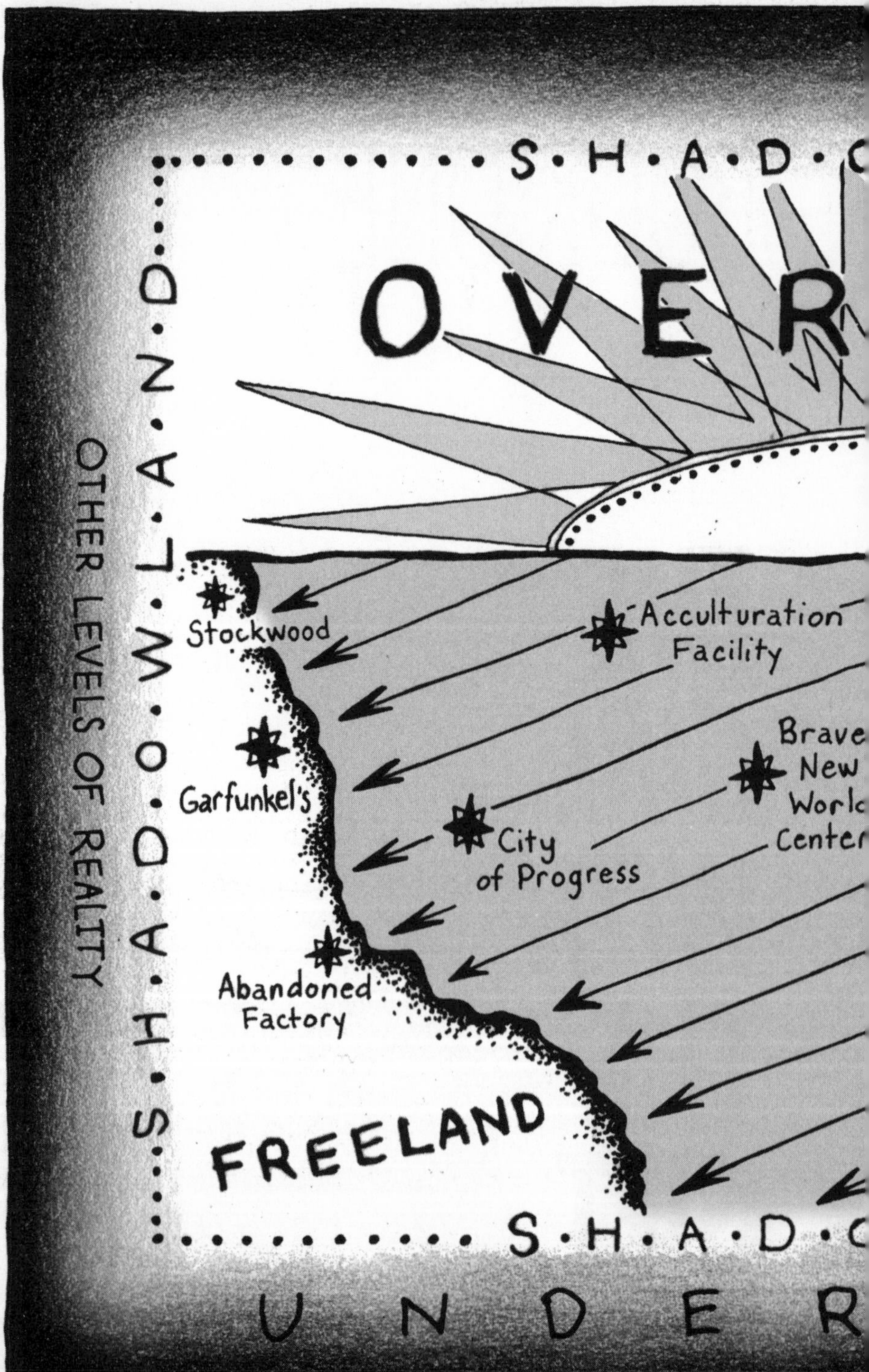
S·H·A·D·O
OVER
Stockwood
Acculturation Facility
Brave New World Center
Garfunkel's
City of Progress
Abandoned Factory
FREELAND
S·H·A·D·O·W·L·A·N·D
OTHER LEVELS OF REALITY
S·H·A·D·O
UNDER

W·L·A·N·D
WORLD
New Order Reformatory/
Overworld Prison
NEW ORDER
CONTROLLED
The
Hospital
The place
we used to
call home
S·H·A·D·O·W·L·A·N·D
OTHER LEVELS OF REALITY
W·L·A·N·D
WORLD

Chapter 1

Whit

LISTEN TO ME. We don't have much time.

My name is Whit Allgood. I guess you've heard of me and my sister, Wisty, and of the crazy stuff that's happened, but here's the thing: *it's so much worse than you think it is.*

Trust me when I tell you that these are *the worst of times* and that the best of times are little more than a distant memory. And no one seems to be paying attention to what's going on. Are *you?*

Paying attention?

Imagine that all the things you love most in the world—and probably take for granted—are now *banned.* Your books, music, movies, art...all snatched away. Burned. That's life under the New Order, the so-called government—or brutal totalitarian regime—that's taken over this world. Now, with every waking breath, we have to fight for every freedom we have left. Even our *imagination* is at risk. Can you picture your government trying to destroy *that?* It's *inhuman.*

And yet... they're calling *us* criminals.

That's right. Wisty and I are the offenders in that unhappy propaganda piece brought to you by the New Order. Our crime? Engaging in free thought and creativity.... Oh, and practicing the "dark and foul arts"—i.e., magic.

Did I lose you? Let me back up a bit.

One night not so long ago, my family was awakened by soldiers storming through our home. Wisty and I were cruelly torn from our parents and slammed into a prison—a death camp for kids. And for what?

They accused us of being a witch and a wizard.

But, the thing is, it turns out the N.O. was actually right about that: we didn't know it at the time, but Wisty and I *do* have powers.

Magic powers. And now we're scheduled to be publicly executed, along with our parents.

That particular ghoulish event hasn't taken place yet — though it will. I promise those of you who crave suspense, adventure, and bloodshed that you can look forward to it. And you *will,* if you're anything like the rest of the brainwashed "citizenry" of our land.

But if you're one of the few who've escaped the N.O.'s clutches, you *need* to hear my story. And Wisty's story. And the story of the Resistance. So when we're gone, there's someone left to spread the word.

Someone to fight the good fight.

And so we begin with the story of *another* public execution: a sad and unfortunate event, an accident, as luck or fate would have it. In a phrase that I hate to use under any circumstances: *a tragedy.*

Chapter 2

Whit

HERE'S WHAT HAPPENED, to the best of my shattered ability to recall it.

I do remember that I couldn't have been more lost and alone as I wandered the streets of this gray, crowded, and forsaken city. *Where is my sister? Where are the others from the Resistance?* I kept thinking, or maybe muttering the words like some homeless madman.

The New Order has already disfigured this once beautiful city beyond recognition. It seems like a decaying corpse swelling with mindless maggots. The suffocatingly low sky, the featureless buildings—even the faces of the nervously rushing people flooding around me—are as colorless and lifeless as the concrete under my feet.

I know the general populace has been efficiently brainwashed by the New Order, but these citizens seem a little *too* hushed, a little *too* urgent, a little *too* riveted to the scraps of propaganda clutched in their hands like prayer books.

Suddenly, my eyes spot a word in bold letters on the paper: EXECUTION.

And then the huge video displays hanging above the boulevard light up, and everything becomes clear to me. Every pedestrian stops and stands stock-still, and every head turns upward as if there has suddenly been an eclipse.

On the video screens, a hooded prisoner—small-framed, frail-looking—is kneeling on a starkly lit stage.

"Wisteria Allgood," blares a bone-chilling voice, "do you wish to confess to the use of the dark arts for the wicked purpose of undermining all that is good and proper in our society?"

This can't be happening. My heart is a big lump in my throat. *Wisty?* Did that voice really just say *Wisteria Allgood?* My sister's on an executioner's scaffold?

I grab a slack-jawed adult by his dismally gray overcoat lapels. "Where is this execution happening? Tell me right now!"

"The Courtyard of Justice." He blinks at me irritably, as if I've woken him from a deep sleep. "Where else?"

"Courtyard of Justice? Where's *that?*" I demand of the man, throwing my hands around his neck, nearly losing control of my own strength. I swear, I'm ready to throw this adult against a wall if I have to.

"Under the victory arch—down there," he gasps. He points at a boulevard that runs off to my left. "Let me go! I'll call the police!"

I shove him and take off running toward a massive ceremonial arch maybe a half mile away.

"You! Wait!" he yells after me. *"Don't I know your face from somewhere?"*

He does. Oh yes. And so would everyone

else, if they took the time to notice that there was a wanted criminal running loose in their midst.

But his fellow citizens' eyes remain glued to the screen. They've got an insatiable appetite for malicious gossip of any kind and, of course, an equal taste for senseless death and destruction.

Even when the falsely condemned are kids. Just kids.

I can hear a distant roar now. The sound of hunger—for "justice," for blood.

I forge ahead into the pathetic herd of lemmings. *I'm not going to let them take my sister from me.* Not without a fight to the death anyway.

I round a corner, and then, across the top of the crowd, I see…*Is that my sister, Wisty, up on the stage?* She's hooded, dressed all in black, but standing now. Proudly. Brave as ever.

A man—if you would call him that—is on the stage with her. He's leaning on a crooked stick, his wickedly sharp black suit hanging strangely motionless in the wind that's begun to howl through the civic square. His angular face is glowing with smug self-satisfaction, as if he's just devoured a potful of whipping cream.

I know him; I despise him. *The One Who Is The One.* Quite possibly the most evil individual in the history of humanity.

Are there minutes or seconds left before this hideous execution? I have no way of knowing.

I knock people aside as I barrel through the thickening, or should I say *sickening,* throng. I can see a line of well-armed soldiers holding everyone back from the platform. If I can knock one of them down and snatch away a gun...

I look up at the stage just in time to see The One raise his knobby black stick and shake it menacingly at my sister. He has a look of absolute triumph.

"No!" I yell, but I'm unheard in the roaring crowd. They all know what's about to happen. I know, too. I just don't see how I can possibly stop it. There has to be a way.

"Nooo!" I scream. *"You can't do this! This is cold-blooded murder!"*

There's a flash—not of light but somehow of *blackness*—and she's gone. Wisty. My sister. My best friend in the world.

My little sister is dead.

Chapter 3

Whit

IF I'M STILL DRAWING air, it's not because I care about living.

The last person in the Allgood family that I knew for certain to be alive, the person who knew me better than anyone else in the world, the person who looked up to me in everything, is *gone*. What an incredible waste of an incredible life.

Wisty died while I watched, and I could do nothing to help her.

The One just vaporized my sister... and that monster, without any hint of conscience, doesn't even seem to have broken a sweat. He throws his arms in the air like he's just scored a goal, like he's mocking the pointlessness of human existence. I go weak in the knees. I feel as if I might throw up as I hear a deafening roar of approval sweep down the concrete canyon of this city—a place that now seems despicable and evil and beyond repair.

The One has just achieved his biggest public relations triumph *ever*. He basks in the adoration—but his usual impatience and anger soon erupt.

"Silence!"

His command sweeps across the city, obliterating every other noise.

But I'm unmoved. Still shell-shocked. Numb everywhere, including in places that I didn't know existed.

"My good citizens," he thunders, without aid of a microphone, "this is a truly magnificent occasion. What you have just witnessed is the obliteration of the last significant threat to our stewardship of the Overworld! Wisteria Allgood, a leader of the Resistance, has just been removed from this dimension. Forever."

He raises his arms again, and a new gust of wind brings a thin layer of ash and the horrible smell of burnt hair across the crowd. These "good citizens" begin cheering again.

I'd collapse to my knees, but I'm surrounded on all sides. Then, suddenly, there is space for me to move. The cheering turns to screaming and the crowd is surging—moving backward—and I see a fiery explosion erupting not fifty yards from where I stand.

I *know* that fire.

"Oh yeah!" I shout as the mere sight of it makes my heart almost burst with joy. *"Oh yeah, oh YEAH!"*

That's my sister! Wisty's alive! She's just set herself on fire, and that, believe it or not, is a good thing.

Chapter 4

Wisty

AS SURE AS I am Wisteria Rose Allgood, I have only one thought: *I'm gonna* burn *everything and everyone around me. Burn it all down.*

I'll start with the death-drenched stage, move on to this ridiculously pompous plaza, then hit the whole cold city of stone — this disastrous nightmare of a world. Even if I fry myself to ash in the process, I am going to obliterate all of this, all of them.

The One Who Is The One just killed my friend Margo up on that stage from hell. I recognized her even with a hood over her head. Her purple sneakers and black-and-purple cargo pants were the giveaway. The silver streaks and stars on the sneakers were the final clue. Margo, the last punk rocker on Earth. Margo, the most fearless and dedicated person I've ever known. Margo, my dear friend.

Don't ask me why that monster in the black silk suit was pretending she was me. All I know is that *I'm going to burn that evil madman to cinders.*

So I turn myself into a human torch, just as I have in the past. Only this time I abandon all caution. Suddenly ten-, twenty-, thirty-foot tongues of flame are coursing around me, ripping upward in the formerly cool afternoon air.

The crowd backs away, screaming, and I can't help myself: I smile. I nearly laugh out loud.

And I'm about to turn the heat up another notch — to send jets of fire everywhere around me, to burn brighter and hotter than ever before — when my breath catches in my throat.

I feel *him*. I feel his wretched, diseased mind. I feel his eyes somehow locking on to me.

A thousand soldiers turn my way in unison, and now it's The One who's smiling. He's starting to laugh. And he's laughing at me.

I wince as the air rushes out of me. *How can he have so much power?*

I have no choice but to run, at least to try to escape his wrath.

I throw myself into the panicked human tide, my small frame deftly ducking elbows and shoulders. But The One is too close. I can feel his icy gusts chasing me, reaching out with cold, bony finger–like wisps, grazing my face, my neck, sending a chill so cold it hurts every-where at once.

I'm starting to think how ironic it is that a firegirl might die in a deep freeze when sud-denly I'm smothered by warmth. Somebody grabs me, lifts me up, and nearly squeezes all the breath out of me.

Chapter 5

Wisty

IT'S MY BROTHER, Whit.

In a flash, he carries me a hundred, two hundred paces ahead, as if I weigh nothing. Then he and I duck behind a high stone wall. For a few precious seconds, we're out of sight and safe.

I hug Whit with all the strength I have. He finally relaxes his powerful grip enough for me to breathe.

"But if this is really *you*..." He trails off.

"Margo," I whisper. "He killed Margo." Then suddenly I'm crying like a baby. I'm shaking, and my teeth chatter hopelessly.

Margo is *dead*. The girl who helped me put a third piercing in my ear last week. The girl who woke us all up at five a.m. every morning to report for duty, the girl who had more dedication to fighting the oppression of the New Order than the rest of us put together. She was so young. Just fifteen years old.

"I told her not to go in that building without more help. I begged her," my brother says. "Why did she go in there? *Why?*"

"She was always the last to give up on a mission," I remind Whit, as if I'm trying to convince myself that it wasn't our fault she'd been caught. "First in, last out. That was her mantra, right? Stupid!"

"Courageous," he says, and for an instant I see in his eyes why it is that girls love him, why *I* love him. He's honest and sincere and absolutely fearless.

The mission, one of a dozen attempted rescues we'd undertaken in the last month, was our worst failure yet. We were trying to liberate maybe a hundred kidnapped kids from a New Order testing facility. But our intelligence must have been off. Instead of victimized kids, the building held a platoon of New Order soldiers. They were waiting for us.

"Actually, it's lucky *any* of us—," I start to say.

"Find her!" The speakers mounted in the plaza start vibrating with The One's irate voice. "There's *another* conspirator in the crowd! She has flaming-red hair! Close the courtyard exits. Capture her *now!*"

Whit grabs a gray hat off a passing businessman and plunks it down on my head.

"Tuck your hair in, quick," he says.

I'm doing just that when a policeman spots me. He's a couple of dozen yards away.

Now he's grabbing for the whistle at the end of a cord around his neck...and he'll soon have the attention of every soldier in the plaza. Not to mention that of The One, whom I *hate* to mention.

But then a small black figure leaps up and knocks the policeman down flat on his rear.

Whit and I exchange looks of surprise. He says, "Did you just—?"

But before Whit can finish, the black figure—an old woman—is at our side. She presses into my hand a crumpled, gritty piece of paper. "Take it, take it!"

I swear she's the weirdest-looking creature I've ever seen in my life, and yet I *know* her from somewhere.

"Who are—?"

She cuts me off. "Follow this. Go! I'm a friend. Run. Run. Don't stop for a single breath, or it's over. For all of us. *Go!*"

Somehow she gets behind us, and then she delivers a kick to both of our butts. That sends us staggering into the surging crowd.

I immediately turn back…but there's no sign of her.

"You heard her," says Whit. "Go! Now! Go!"

Chapter 6

Wisty

THE CRUMPLED, quintuple-folded paper the old woman had forced into my hand is a map. *She said she was a friend, right? Besides, what better plan do we have?* So Whit and I follow the map.

The dotted line on the dirty, handwritten piece of parchment leads us through the south side of the city. So far, so safe and alive.

"I can't place her," I muse as we hike outside the city's perimeter toward a set of railroad tracks. "Was she...maybe one of Mom and Dad's friends?"

Whit shrugs. "Doesn't matter, does it? Any person willing to risk her life tackling a New

Order policeman is a friend. A really *good* friend."

Whit rips down a NOTICE from a loud-speaker post near the track and tears it into shreds. "By the way, when did you become a *'leader of the Resistance'?*" he asks with a chuckle and a glint of his baby blues.

"Hey, if The One says it's so..."

"Leave it to you to be launched into fame and fortune by a totalitarian thug."

"Shut up!" I start chasing him down the track, laughing in spite of myself. "You're just jealous!" And Whit starts pumping his arms into a sprint, back in football mode.

"No fair!" I call after him. He's bigger and older, and of course he can run faster. A lot faster.

For just a few minutes, we let ourselves be kids again. A brother and sister racing along the train tracks. Pretending that one of their best friends hadn't just been murdered, that they weren't on the run from half the world.

With a burst of enthusiasm, maybe even fun, we run those last few miles to our destination—a little brick building that appears on the map with an X and the instruction: GO THROUGH SIGNAL HUT.

"You have *keys?*" I yell to Whit, noting the chain and padlock on the door.

"You have *spells?*" he calls back.

Oh yeah—that's right. I'm a witch. And Whit's a wizard.

Sometimes it's hard to remember things like that when you're busy running for your life. But I *do* have spells—and they do seem to occasionally work on chains and padlocks.

And pretty soon we've actually escaped from the fiends of the N.O.

For the moment anyway.

Chapter 7

HE IS SURROUNDED BY a dozen or more famous works of art that he's had confiscated—works by the likes of Pepe Pompano, Pondrian, Cezonne, Feynoir—the best of the best. All banned and forbidden. All his now.

"Bring me The One Who Commands The Hunt," bellows The One. He can't take much more of this incompetence, this stupidity, this repeated *almost* capturing of Wisteria Allgood and the very, very potent *Gift* that she possesses.

As if on cue, the hunt commander appears in the doorway, looking—despite his gray hair and middle-aged paunch—like a dim student who has just arrived for a midterm he hasn't studied for.

"You failed to capture Wisteria Allgood. Is that correct? Is that true?"

The commander nervously clears his throat.

"Yes, sir," he agrees. He's heard unsettling stories of citizens who have tried to defend themselves in similar situations with The One.

"And would you say today's spectacle was anything short of a public relations disaster? I honestly want to hear your opinion."

"Well, you did execute the other witch in a most decisive fashion, Your Excellency. The citizenry was uplifted by—"

"*She wasn't a witch!* She was just a friend of the witch. Actually she was *bait* for the real witch."

"Well, but…still…she was a valued member of the Resistance, and your destruction of her was magnificent and uplifting to the public in its awe-inspir—"

"The One Who Makes Up The News is going to have her work cut out with tonight's broadcast. Do you have any good ideas about that? How we explain that we executed Wisteria Allgood and then, moments later, we suddenly happened to be chasing another red-haired teenage witch through the city plaza? Be honest. Be forthright. Be quick."

"Umm, well—"

"Silence!" yells The One in a stentorian voice that seems to make the building shake.

The next pause is deadly, truly deadly, and seems to suck all the air out of the room.

Now The One sighs and finally smiles, if you can call it that. "Well, I suppose it could have been worse." His suddenly bright tone entirely belies the anger from just seconds before. "Tell me, Commander, do I recall that all you huntsmen enjoy cigars? I'm sure that's correct. Is it correct?"

"Why, um, yes, thank you," stammers the commander. He briefly wonders how he so suddenly has stumbled into his leader's good graces. He accepts a very fine cigar. And then—a light.

"I've always been fascinated with fire, Commander. . . . Have *you*?"

But the soldier doesn't have a chance to answer.

The glowing red ember at the tip of his cigar quickly expands. It runs up the entire length, then across the man's face, over the back of his skull, and down his neck. Then the bright red, smoldering line races around and around his torso and arms, down to the tips of his toes—leaving the hunt commander, for the briefest moment, a statue of ash.

Then The One taps his cane lightly on the ground, and the gray powder collapses in a soft plume of smoke.

"You failed to capture Wisteria Allgood, and failure isn't an option in this Brave New World."

Chapter 8

Whit

WOULD YOU THINK that I was completely mad if I told you that what saved us in that signal hut was a *portal* that sucked me and Wisty through several dimensions and hurled us back into our current hellish reality at a completely different location?

A year ago, I would've checked myself into a psych ward for that, but *crazy* is the new *sane* in a society defined by New Order nutjobs. FYI, a portal is one of these elusive spots where the fabric of this world is...soft. But stepping through one can be anything *but*. It can hurl you into an entirely different place, time, or dimension...or sometimes force you into places you'd rather not be. Violently.

Like, for instance, in this cramped pitch-black space we've landed in. For all I know, we might be locked in The One's shoe closet. The air feels close, stale. My shoulder's on fire and my head is pounding.

"Whit? Are you here?" I hear a whisper. There's a gentle shifting around about a dozen feet away.

"Yeah." I grunt, half dazed by pain. The sweet female voice is warm, soothing.

"You okay?" the voice asks with concern. *Celia?* I imagine my long-lost girlfriend, kidnapped and killed by the New Order a lifetime ago. Coming closer, leaning over me, about to touch me, heal me, save me...

"Mmmmmm..." I trail off, waiting for Celia's scent, her arms around me.

"You sound...*hungover.*"

Oh. It's Wisty. Of course.

I groan. "It's my shoulder. Got dislocated in the portal, I think."

"Seriously? I slipped right through that one like butter."

I roll my eyes even though she probably can't see them. "Guess it was just the right size

32

for your runty witch butt," I croak out—affectionately, I swear. "So where d'you think we are?"

"How about…a prison? Seems like our favorite crib these days."

I wasn't so sure. "No. This smell—it's not the smell of a prison. It's something…good. Something that reminds me of…"

"Home," we both say in unison.

Wisty releases a small flame from her fingertip to give us some light. I'm impressed at how she's learning to control her hot little temper and putting her talent to good use. In the old days, I used to be the accomplished star around town—MVP varsity football player, plus a top-ranked runner and swimmer—while Wisty was mostly cutting class. Now she's this hotshot witch who can glow, morph, zap, and do other cool stuff. Just not necessarily on command.

In the dim light I see just enough to make out my sister's shape and stacks of cardboard boxes labeled INCINERATE. "Books," Wisty says reverently, paging through a few volumes from unsealed boxes. With my good arm I gingerly poke into a crate and spy titles by all kinds of famous authors, from B. B. White to Roy Royce.

"Looks like a book-burning shipment," I guess. The New Order is in the process of destroying just about every known book in the occupied Overworld written before the takeover.

A stabbing pain rips through my bad shoulder, and I wince. "Speaking of burning...you gonna help me pop my shoulder back in, Wist?"

"That's positively revolting," she says, but makes her way over to me anyway. "You need to learn a spell for that, Brother. You wizard types are supposed to be good at that kind of stuff, right?"

"It's worth a shot, I guess. Just give me a hand with my journal, okay?" Dad gave me this blank book before we were taken away that awful night so many months ago, and I carry it with me everywhere. (Wisty carts around an old drumstick/wand that Mom gave her.) Most of the time my book's blank and I use it to write in — usually sad love poems for Celia. But sometimes it fills with magazines, maps, whole works of literature... or, if we're lucky, spells. I think wizards are supposed to be able to control what comes when, but so far it's basically a crapshoot.

Wisty takes it out of my pack and helps me flip through the pages for any sort of injury-healing spell, and we finally come up with this mouthful: *Voron klaktu scapulati.*

"Sounds like *devilspeak* to me!" Wisty quips, impersonating a crotchety old lady talking about rock music. But the most amazing warmth spreads through my shoulder when I say it, and suddenly — just like that — it's back in its socket. I raise my arm without a twinge of pain.

"Guess we've sold our souls," I say. "Now let's figure out where the heck we are and how to get back to Freeland."

As we make our way to the rear of the cramped space, we figure out we're inside a shipping container. I grab a few books for the kids back at Resistance headquarters — *The Blueprints of Bruno Genet* and *The Thirst Tournament,* among others.

"You ready to face what's out there?" I ask as we reach the door.

"Or *who's* out there," Wisty echoes warily. "Lemme get focused, in case I have to light up or something."

On the count of three, we roll up the container door.

And there, staring right at us, are... *our parents.*

Chapter 9

Whit

WELL, AT LEAST it's their *heads* anyway.

Our parents' photos are on a twenty-foot bill-board, their faces looking lost and lonely in this abandoned rail yard. And below their mug shots are words that never cease to chill our bones:

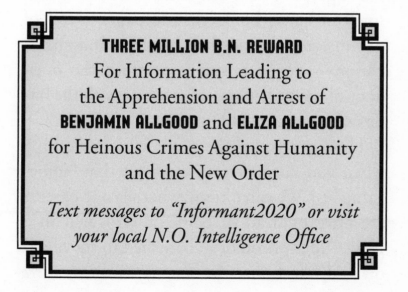

THREE MILLION B.N. REWARD
For Information Leading to
the Apprehension and Arrest of
BENJAMIN ALLGOOD and **ELIZA ALLGOOD**
for Heinous Crimes Against Humanity
and the New Order

*Text messages to "Informant2020" or visit
your local N.O. Intelligence Office*

Sure, we *know* our parents are wanted criminals—for the same bogus reasons we are. But having it in black and white for all the world to see—and slapping the pathetic price of three million beans on their heads!—is a cruel reminder that this nightmare may never come to a happy end.

Wisty, as usual, reads my mind and throws me a semihopeful bone. "They're still free," she points out quietly.

"At least they *were*," I say, "whenever this poster was put up." The paper does look a little weathered—faded, frayed, and even torn at the edges. We both fall silent as the powerful smell of aging books' brittle pages—full of dreams, stories, tragedies, laughter, and imagination—seems to swirl out from the open door of the trailer and smother us with the bittersweet memory of home.

How can you make peace with something when you don't even know what that "something" is? We can't know whether our parents are alive or dead or being interrogated in a New Order prison or...banished to the Shadowland like Celia. *Are they suffering? Is there anything we can do about it? Or are we as help-less and useless as I feel right now?*

I punch the billboard so hard my fist goes right through the pressboard backing.

Then I pull my hand out and try to pretend it didn't happen. Wisty gives me a concerned look, and I shrug. I'm sure my knuckles are bleeding, but I don't feel a thing.

I glance at her worried, grief-strained face and quickly look away. I have an urge to hug her, but I need to show her that I'm not letting my emotions take over. I swallow a golf ball–size lump in my throat and take Wisty's hand. "Let's get out of here."

There are no people on the outskirts of this eerie town. Just broken windows in ware-houses. Streets strewn with rubble. The only new construction appears to be enormous video billboards and loudspeaker towers.

As we make our way to the town center, I imagine what it might have once been like here. Quaint. I see a redbrick high school, jungle gyms, a park with a gazebo, an over-turned tricycle. A pang of sadness grips me. It reminds me of our old town—church steeples, neighborhood grocery stores, and actual *trees*.

Now I'm even more homesick. For Mom, Dad, home — even school. A little.

"I wonder where everybody is," Wisty whispers.

"I don't," I answer, maybe a little too quickly. "I mean... I don't really *want* to know."

And then I hear this: *"You don't?... don't?... don't?... don't?... Why, Whit?"*

I whirl my head around. Wisty stares at me.

There was definitely a voice. And it wasn't Wisty's. Or mine.

It was Celia's voice.

Maybe this is a ghost town. *Literally.*

Chapter 10

Whit

I'M OFF LIKE a missile to find her. It's as if I don't even have a choice. As if this is my fate.

"Celia!" I run through barren streets, past empty shops, a police station with no police, a boarded-up middle school, a movie theater.... I don't see her, or anyone else actually. Everything seems so unreal here. *Is it real? Am I dreaming up all of this desolation?*

"Celia!"

"Whit, wait!" I hear Wisty's voice coming from behind. The slapping of her sneakers against pavement. She's trying to keep up.

"Stop! Whit, please! You don't know it's her! It could be a trap!"

I *do* know it's her. You never, ever forget the voice of the one you love. Whether it's a whisper or a scream or a distant memory, I know when it's Celia. I guess Wisty doesn't understand that. She's never been in love.

And then I hear Celia again. But not from too far away. It feels as if she's all around me somehow.

"You don't want to *know?*...know?... know?...What *happened* to us?...us?... us?..."

I can't stand it—*Celia feels so close now.*

Her voice is so loud that it's as if she's broadcasting right into my head. It's unbearable... but also the most beautiful, incredible kind of pain. Torture I'd beg for. Does that make any sense?

"I *do!* I do want to know!" I halt in my tracks, then I sink to my knees in the middle of the town square. "Where are you, Celes? *I need to see you again.*"

"Look *up,* Whit. She's right there."

It's Wisty's voice, to my left. And when I raise my head, I see what she sees.

There is my girlfriend—on-screen. *Celia,*

on a New Order propaganda board. Her gorgeous face is more than twice my height, and every inch of it is as smooth and perfect and beautiful as I remember it. It's as if she's a movie star.

Chapter 11

Whit

"DID YOU FORGET about us, Whit? Did you forget about me?" Celia looks sad, making this even more painful for me. "I guess I can't blame you for moving on."

"What are you talking about, Celia? I never forget you. Everybody knows that. I never stop thinking about you, trying to find you. People think I'm crazy!"

"Maybe you haven't totally forgotten me, Whit. But I'm talking about *us*. The lost, the kidnapped, the murdered. The Half-lights." I shiver at her mention of the sad souls in the Shadowland. "I'm really not...*me* anymore. I'm part of something...bigger."

"Celia, you'll always be you. The Shadowland can't destroy you. Not for me. Where are you? The *real* you—?"

"You don't get it, Whit." Celia breaks into my words and smiles wistfully. "I've got to give you credit, baby. You really are the most sensitive football hero who ever walked the face of this world. But you're like a lot of guys in other ways, Whit. You're such a boy. You see and care about and protect only what's right in front of you."

"No." I shake my head in disbelief at her words. "That's not true. You know it isn't."

Why is she trying to hurt me?

"Yes, it is," Celia says, her eyes boring into mine. "Case in point. Where's your sister?"

I whirl around in a three-sixty. Wisty is...

Gone?

"What the...?" I start tearing around the square, looking down alleyways frantically. *"Wisty!"*

This can't be. Has she been kidnapped?

"You have to start thinking bigger, Whit." It's torture—Celia's voice is coursing through me like a living force, and all I want to do is capture it, surrender to it. But my sister...

"I know you're scared," she goes on, strangely unmoved by Wisty's disappearance. "You just lost someone you cared about, and you don't know how to deal with it. Think about that, Whit. It's the key."

"Wisty!" I scream. The only response is the whisking sound of an empty plastic bag skimming across the town square.

"Whit—*up here. Look at me.* I'm here to tell you more that you don't want to hear. You and Wisty need to stop running away from the New Order. Stop running from The One."

"Never! I'm going to find Wisty, and we're going back to the Shadowland—to find you. Not an image on a screen!"

Celia's thick, wavy black hair starts streaming out, tickling her lips. Almost as if it's responding to the wind in the plaza. The plastic bag blows into my face. I tear it away in frustration.

"Whit, are you listening to me? Do I need to get any louder?"

My head will explode if she does. "I can

hear you, trust me. You're just not making sense at the moment."

"You and Wisty need to turn yourselves in, to save your parents—and the rest of us. It's the only way. I think Wisty understands that...right, Wisty?"

Celia turns her head, and there—behind her, *up on the screen*—is my sister. *How can that be?*

"Wisty!" I yell. "How—?"

"It's okay, Whit," Wisty says. "Everything is okay now. I understand our role."

Celia looks back at me, and her long hair starts *reaching out of the screen,* flowing toward me. I feel pulled in by it. I have no resistance to her. I feel as if I'm airborne, flying toward the screen to be swallowed by her eyes, her lips, her soft, soothing voice.

"I have to go now, Whit. Turn yourselves in. Save us. You can do this, Whit."

Then the screen fuzzes out, and I'm falling into blackness that seems to have no end.

Chapter 12

Wisty

NOW THAT WAS MAYBE the strangest thing that has happened to us so far. Another mystery inside a mystery inside a mystery.

I remember almost nothing. At least, nothing after I told Whit to look up at the screen — and Celia. Now I'm flat on my face in the middle of the town plaza, and my head is pounding.

I turn to find Whit in a similar state, only he's holding his head with both hands and sobbing. There's not much that's worse than seeing your older brother cry. Except maybe seeing your parents that way.

I scramble over to him and hold him as he tells me what happened. It's a pretty incoherent jumble, but one thing is clear: Celia said we had to turn ourselves in. *Nice one, Celes. I'll chew on that. First let's go over your connection to the New Order one more time. How did you get up on the propaganda board?*

"We're not turning ourselves in," I tell him dismissively. "It's a video trick. The N.O. is getting desperate."

"It's BS!" he says indignantly, suddenly straightening. "I know it now. That wasn't Celia talking. It couldn't have been. We're going to destroy this regime, and we can't do it if we're prisoners. Or dead."

I pull myself up. "Wow," I say, brushing the dust off. "Got knocked back by charging testosterone, there."

Whit manages to laugh at my lame joke, then surprises me with a fake bull charge, shoulder to gut.

"Yeah! We're gonna take 'em down!" he yells.

"Yee-ha!" a bunch of little voices shout. *What now?*

We turn and see the most ragamuffiny band of ragamuffins poking their heads out of the doorway of a boarded-up video-game store.

"Who are you?" I ask, wide-eyed. They're clearly not so nervous that they don't want to be seen, but not so trusting that they want to be in arm's reach.

One little boy with an incredible burr-tangled mane of brown-blond hair steps forward.

"Are you guys *regular* people?" he asks. He can't be much past the third grade.

"If you mean we're *not* brainwashed by the New Order, yeah," I say. "We're not. Where are your parents?"

"They're gone. We don't know where. Taken."

"Taken?"

"The soldiers put them in trucks and stole 'em away," he says. Some of the smaller boys and girls start to rub tears from their eyes.

A flash of emotion crosses Whit's face. Sympathy, empathy—call it what you will. My brother's not exactly a softy, except when he ought to be. He takes off his knapsack and puts it on the ground in front of him, then rests his hands on it for a moment with his eyes closed.

And then—it's the most surreal thing—a puppy and two kittens poke their heads out of the bag.

The children's sorrow turns to wonder and laughter as the puppy and kittens scamper out of the bag. The kids who can't get in to pet the animals are looking back at Whit with awe. Frankly, so am I. *"Whoa!"* I say.

Now he's pulling back on his collar, and white doves are fluttering out of his shirt and up into the sky. And now—gross!—he sneezes and a cloud of yellow bees comes out of his nose and zooms up after the doves. The kids are laughing hysterically.

"Where'd you learn the parlor tricks?" I ask Whit. "Sweet. You're becoming a rather charming wizard."

He shrugs. "I thought I should do something nice for someone else for a change, instead of just worrying about us all of the time," he says, and turns back to the merrymaking kids. "You guys want to come with us?" he offers.

Wow. The things that can happen when you black out for a few minutes. Suddenly my brother's become Mr. Whitford Fountain-of-Charity Allgood, Esq.

"You gonna open a soup kitchen next?" I say with a big smile.

"Maybe," he says. "Why not?" And then my brother conjures up a big pot of hot tomato soup, with bowls and spoons, and just the right amount for everybody.

Chapter 13

Wisty

WITH THE HELP OF some spells that appear in Whit's journal, we're able to find our way back to Garfunkel's department store, which thankfully is only several miles away. But trying to dodge New Order surveillance with a stream of dirty, chattering kids in tow is no picnic, let me tell you. I'm never becoming a camp counselor.

As we stride in, the first thing I notice from the back of the crowd—where I'm rounding up stray kids like a kindergarten teacher's aide—is Janine. She's our most reliable Freeland icon after Margo. Her eyes light up brightly as she runs past the empty cosmetics counters to welcome her hero.

My brother, Whit, that is. In case I haven't mentioned this enough, a lot of girls adore Whit. Which, I guess, makes his faithfulness to Celia kind of extra impressive.

"You *did* it!" Janine clutches him before he has a chance to explain that these kids aren't the ones we were *supposed* to rescue. "This is way beyond our expectations! We didn't think—"

Whit gently pushes her away, pain in his eyes. "It's not that simple, Janine." Next, Feffer, our rescued hound, comes prancing up, barking with excitement.

"Where's Margo?" Sasha, our resident zealot, asks with confusion all over his face.

Oh God. They think we succeeded on our original mission. They don't know...

And so, for the next fifteen minutes, utter devastation drowns the group as we explain the sordid outcome of the mission that failed.

Margo was one of the original and most beloved Freeland leaders, one of the real rocks in our ever-changing existence. As it turns out, those on the mission who had escaped got back to Freeland without witnessing her execution.

And Garfunkel's—whose power mostly comes from an ingenious method of siphoning energy from perfume bottles—doesn't have regular access to New Order broadcasts. Actually, that's probably a blessing.

"We were all just keeping vigil for your return," Sasha says. "For *all* of you."

Having to tell the story just tears me up all over again. And looking around at everyone makes it worse. The ragamuffin crew's light of hope seems extinguished. I'm even sorry for Sasha, whom I don't particularly trust because he lied through his teeth to us once. But he and Margo had the same fire of resistance in their blood. They would do anything for the cause.

And Janine—well, she and Margo were like sisters. Her green eyes, which had shone so brightly for Whit, were glazed over with shock and grief. Whit was stroking her hair comfortingly. Finally, she buried her head in the crook of his neck. "We grew up together," she moaned. "Best friends since preschool, you believe that?"

"Sure I do," whispers Whit. "Everybody loved Margo."

Emmet, my best bud here, comes over to me and puts his arm around me. Normally it would make me beyond happy — because, let's face it, Emmet is extremely wicked cute — but right now, strangely, it almost annoys me.

I've had it with falling apart. If Margo walked in here right now, she would probably revolt against all this pitiful weeping and feeling sorry for her.

A revolt. Not a bad idea actually.

"Look!" I say, sliding away from Emmet's arm and climbing on top of a glass makeup counter. "The hankie festival is over. The last thing Margo would want is to see us sitting around moping." Sasha nods. "We have to keep moving; we have to stay ready. The New Order is just getting stronger."

Jamilla, our "team mother" shaman, dries the tears on her cheeks. Even Feffer shows a little more of the steely glint she usually has in her eyes.

"The One Who Is The One wants to crush our spirit!" I yell. "Would Margo have let her spirit be crushed?"

"No!" Sasha yells back. "Absolutely not."

"The One Who Is The One wants us to stop, to turn ourselves in, to quit!" I shout. "Did Margo ever stop resisting?"

"No!" a group of us says in unison.

"The One Who Is The One doesn't want us to execute our next mission. And the one after that. Would Margo have told us to execute our next mission?"

"Yes!" Almost the whole room's on board now.

Then Emmet—who's looking maybe even cuter than usual—stands up with his fist in the air. The volume in the room grows, and I'm definitely feeling giddy. Maybe there really is something to this leadership stuff.

But then something happens to let all the wind out of my sails.

The person I detest the most in the whole world has just entered the room.

Well, maybe not quite the *most.* But darn close.

Chapter 14

Wisty

BYRON TRAITOR SUCK-UP P. Weasel Swain skulks into the room, bobbing his head like an animal trying to pick up a scent, and then makes a beeline for me. Byron was a know-it-all snob in high school and then a New Order puppet who was complicit in our capture—and who, by the way, I actually turned into a weasel once. He has supposedly left the N.O., but that doesn't mean I have to like him.

"Hey, everybody!" he yells in his permanently annoying, ratty little voice. Then he climbs up next to me on the counter. I should turn him back into a weasel so I can put him in a box, wrap it in duct tape, and mail it to the General Bowen State Psychiatric Hospital. *Without* a supply of his icky hair product.

"I guess you haven't heard the bad news, Byron," Jamilla begins tentatively.

"Oh, indeed I have," he says. *Who talks like that?* "Seen it with my own eyes." Everyone gasps. "On this."

He pulls out a top-of-the-line smartphone that he's gotten from who knows where, swipes it a few times, then holds up the device with the screen facing the group.

Oh God, it's the Courtyard of Justice, where Margo's hooded figure is seen kneeling before The One.

"Put it away," I snap at him, reaching for the phone. "That's a snuff film."

"Absolutely not!" Byron shouts, tightening his grip. "They *need* to see it."

"You are truly horrific!" I screech, practically clawing at his hands for it. But Byron, being weaselly, is an artful dodger, and I have to attack him like a lioness to get my hands on the thing.

"Wisty," Janine says out of the blue, steely and determined as she pulls away from Whit's comforting arms. "He's right. I need to see it. What they did to her."

I exchange a defeated glance with Whit and step to another counter so I don't have to be so close to Weasel Boy. He holds the phone up triumphantly, and though I try to turn away, I can't.

In the most stomach-turning slow-motion replay I've ever seen, we watch Margo's complete disintegration by The One Who Is The One. Her hood, her clothes, the skin of her hands, her wonderful sneakers, turn gray for an instant and then she just kind of comes apart, billowing away in a puff of crematory ash.

"You see," he explains as the footage continues, "they want everyone to believe Wisty is dead. So, because of my connections high up at the Ministry of Information—my father, to be precise—I was able to hack into their system and share some truth with the world."

I look closely. He's evidently got his weaselly hands on a broadcast from Channel One Who Is The One—*and changed it.* The caption accompanying the footage now reads: THE PERSON EXECUTED HERE WAS NOT WISTERIA ALLGOOD BUT AN INNOCENT GIRL NAMED MARGO. THIS WAS A MURDER.

The screen cuts back to the totally annoyed news anchor. "People of the New Order," she says, "as you can see, a small group of terrorists is attempting to undermine our broadcasts. Pay no attention to that absurd caption under the pictures. We are getting unequivocal verification from the Office of Executions that the public enemy seen here is indeed *Wisteria Allgood.*"

Now Byron's manipulated caption reads: IF IT IS WISTERIA ALLGOOD, WHY IS SHE IN A HOOD SO WE CAN'T SEE HER FACE?

The newscaster puts her finger to her earpiece—clearly her producer or producers are urgently advising her about what to do next.

"Citizens of the New Order," she continues, "the Office of Executions wishes all to note that the single reason Wisteria Allgood is in a hood is that witches cannot cast spells when they have hoods over their heads."

Byron smiles smugly. Another caption appears under the newscaster: LIAR! WE CAN SEE IT IN YOUR EYES.

Whit and I are speechless. My brother actually looks impressed with Byron's efforts, while I'm thinking he just ruined my chances of hiding from all the New Order–loving neighborhood snitches.

I launch another lioness attack, and Whit catches me just in time.

"Stay out of my life, you creep! Did it ever occur to you that I might be perfectly *happy* to be presumed dead?"

"I say way to go, Byron baby," Sasha cuts in smoothly. "You looking to be our leader of the week anytime soon?"

"Over my dead body." I glare at Sasha. He'd been referring to the Freeland tradition of appointing leaders for one week at a time — to avoid the corruption that power usually brings.

"I highly recommend you get over it, Wisty," says Mr. Patronizing. "You're all lead characters in the New Order's most wanted prime-time public-informant program. He's now got photos of everybody from the raids—including Janine, Jamilla, Emmet, and Sasha."

Silence. Janine finally asks the question on everyone's mind. "How...?"

"Those displays we see out on the streets in their part of the Overworld? They're *two*-way. If you're looking at one of his newscasts, chances are he's looking at you, too."

"That's impossible," Whit says, dismissing Byron's idea.

"You doubt me? Then check *this* out," he says. "Not only is he all over the New Order broadcasts, he's making his way into *our* transmissions. Look."

Byron snaps a picture of himself with the phone. I grab it and look at the image. My jaw drops. In the picture, The One Who Is The One's face is *directly over Byron's shoulder.*

"It's probably just proof that you're a traitor," I say, handing back the phone.

"Oh yeah?" snarls Byron. "Then why does it happen with *everybody?*" He turns and snaps a picture of Whit.

Whit takes the phone and looks at the photo of himself. And promptly turns white. He starts to shiver, and this little tic he has in his left eye starts up.

"You *see?*" Byron squeals.

Whit shakes his head and passes the phone back to me. He's shaking all over now; the facial tic is getting worse.

And I see why: it's not The One Who Is The One in the photograph. It's Celia.

The One has Celia.

Chapter 15

Whit

MY TEMPLES ARE POUNDING, and the edges of my vision swirl. My heart feels as if it's trying to climb up into my throat. *I have to find her.* Have to get back to the Shadowland. Need to be swallowed by Celia's beautiful eyes, her hair, her scent. I have to *merge* with her at least one more time.

I leave the phone in my sister's hands, push through the others, and take off running toward the store's loading dock. There's a portal there, a portal I've promised Wisty I'd never take alone.

That's unfortunate, but I *need* this—I need Celia. I have no free will in this matter.

I charge toward the portal wall at a sprint,

figuring if it's been closed off since I was last here, it will serve me right to run full-speed into brick and mortar, maybe knock some sense into me.

It gives, but traveling the portal is like swimming through stone. It feels like an impossible task to break through, but finally I'm soaking in the vaguely familiar, penetrating dark and cold of the Shadowland.

It's an extraordinarily bizarre place between realities, full of wandering Half-lights — souls of the dead who are stuck here, who can sometimes find their way through to a world but who can't stay for long. *Like ghosts slipping in and out of purgatory,* I think to myself.

"Celia!" I yell at the top of my voice. "Celia, it's me! Whit! I'm right here."

I want to be everywhere at once, to bridge the vastness and strangeness of this place in an instant. The problem is that keeping your bearings in the Shadowland is like getting oriented in the middle of an ocean on a bleak and foggy day. Without a GPS. Or a compass. And maybe with a bucket over your head.

I can't allow myself to get lost. But I don't

know where to go. *"Ce-li-a!"* I turn and yell in another direction. Wandering away from the portal could be disastrous. I've never been here alone before. I've been warned against it.

This time I get a response.

Only it's not the response I've been aching for. It's a terrible moan that makes my heart feel as if it's been skewered by an icicle.

The moan trails off, and then there's another one, even louder, closer.

Disaster. I've attracted the attention of Lost Ones — less-than-angelic humans who have been in the Shadowland so long that they've become like rotting souls. Like monsters, I suppose.

I turn and feel around for the way out. *Where is the portal?*

I can't find it — there's just this cold, damp fog everywhere.

They're getting even closer. I can feel their cold and smell their mustiness. *Think! Think! Think!*

I definitely see something moving toward me. A dark shape in the fog — low, limping, searching. I spin a quarter turn to my left —

and there's another disturbance in the mist…
or three…or *six.*

This could be the end for sure.

Another quarter turn—the portal's got to
be in front of me, or maybe just a bit to the
left—

There—I can feel something, or…

Ooomf.

I'm on the ground. On my back. Without
my breath. Then I hear fabric tearing. My
shirt?

My eyes are open, but all I can make out are
the terrible shapes, figures made of flesh but
also smoke. A dozen cold hands are upon me,
restraining me as if I'm on an operating table.

*Am I on an operating table? What in God's
name do they want?*

What is that snapping sound? That sensation in my shoulder? I feel as if my flesh is
being pulled, pushed, *torn,* even. It doesn't
hurt, though. *Am I too cold? Or in shock?*

All I see for certain are wicked, broken, jag-
ged teeth.

I tell myself not to, but I can't help it: I
scream. "Celia!" I wail, realizing this will

probably be the last thing I'll ever say. "I love you!"

They've pinned me down. They're biting me. *They're* eating *me, aren't they?*

But then I hear a new noise through the fog. *Can it be?*

A *bark!*

"Feffer!" I shout. And the biting stops. Or, at least, it pauses. Do the Lost Ones sense the dog? Another piece of fresh meat for them?

I look at the gaping wraith faces as they cast glowing yellow eyes around for the source of the noise. One of them starts moaning again. I look into its shadow-planed face and I recognize who it is. I'm in shock.

Am I hallucinating, or is it the traitor of all traitors—Tall Jonathan?

Jonathan was a Freelander who'd betrayed one of our most important missions. Wisty almost died because of him. For a moment, it makes me almost happy to see him as a creature of ravenous evil.

"Jonathan?" I say, but then he's retreated into the mist. There's a frenzy of furious moaning and snarling to my left. Either Feffer's on the attack or the poor dog is making her last stand. The next thing I know, a large brown shape is tugging at my tattered shirt.

"Feff!" I gasp as Jonathan resurfaces and lunges toward me again, along with a half dozen other horrifying shadow creatures who seem to be drooling.

I stagger after the fearless dog, and though I've never been more glad to be alive, I almost hesitate as Feffer plunges back through the portal.

Where is Celia?

Chapter 16

Whit

IF YOU'VE EVER BEEN AWAKENED by a mysterious crash in the middle of the night, you know the sensation of adrenaline that was pumping through me the second I became conscious. My body's horsepower was revving at about four hundred. I'm talking luxury sports car, here.

I'm not sure, but I guess that's how Janine ended up on the floor next to me, flat on her back.

Apparently, she'd been putting bandages and wraps on my arm, and the sensation of the tight grip freaked me out. *Reaction?* I involuntarily flipped and pinned her to the floor.

Obviously Feffer must have saved me in the Shadowland, but that's the last thing I remembered. Until right about now.

"Oh God," I say. "Sorry, Janine. I thought you were a Lost One. That I was still in the Shadowland. Are you okay?"

"What, you think I can't handle a takedown? I'm fine." Janine props herself up on her hands. "You, on the other hand, are not."

I glance at my arm. "This? It'll heal."

"Your arm might, sure. But…" Janine's brow furrows. "There are other parts of you that are seriously hurt. Damaged, maybe beyond repair. Your *heart,* Whit."

Totaled, I think. Decimated, even. I don't argue with her on that score.

She goes back to her Nurse Janine routine with the wraps. "Everyone knows it's a suicide mission to go to the Shadowland alone—at least not without a *lot* of experience or a trick to find your way back. Wisty and I are pretty upset with you. Do you know how much your sister loves you?"

"I'm fine." This sounds hollow, even to me.

"Going on a suicide mission is *not* fine. We

need you. *I* need you. Does that...mean *anything* to you?"

"It does. I swear it does, Janine. I'm sorry I've been so..." The word Celia had used escapes me now.

"Self-absorbed?" Janine finally smiles. "That's okay. Happens to the best of us, I guess."

"Celia told me to think about the bigger picture. But sometimes I can't think of anything else...but her." I know it's not a great idea to say this in front of Janine.

But she doesn't even flinch. "Tell me about it. About how you're dealing with it, I mean." She finishes with the wrap and levels her eyes at me.

"Well...I don't really know how to talk about it, where to start. Celia disappeared back in our hometown, and suddenly there was this gaping hole in my chest. In my life. We did everything together, and then she was gone."

Janine notices my journal nearby. "Maybe try to write about it, instead of talking."

"Actually, I do. I've got..." *Should I tell her?* "A poem." I laugh nervously. "It's nothing. Dumb."

"A poem?" Janine looks startled. "Can I... hear it?"

"Umm... I don't think—"

"Please, Whit. It would mean a lot to me."

"Okay," I concede. "I guess. But you have to promise you won't tell *anybody*—especially my sister. This is between us."

"I swear," she promises. I trust her more than anybody but Wisty. Janine is actually a very sweet person.

But still, I can't believe I'm reading this to her.

Methought that joy and health alone could be
Where I was not—and pain and sorrow here.
And is it thus?—it is as I foretold,
And shall be more so; for the mind recoils
Upon itself, and the wrecked heart lies cold....
We feel benumbed, and wish to be no more....

As I finish, Janine is gazing thoughtfully. I'm not sure if she likes it or hates it. But then I think I see that her eyes are damp.

"You okay?" I ask. I reach out and touch her arm. Her skin is soft, warm.

"It's so . . . beautiful," she says, wiping away a tear with her sleeve. "Not dumb at all. Definitely not dumb."

And the next thing I know, Wisty's stepping out from behind a clothing rack. "That's a *Lady Myron* poem," she says incredulously. "That is, if I'm recalling Ms. Magruder's eighth-grade English class correctly."

Chapter 17

Wisty

WHIT'S FACE IS so red that I actually feel a little bad about what I just said.

"Umm," I mumble. "Sorry to interrupt."

I really should've clapped my hands on my ears and walked away when Whit started talking about poetry. But to miss Whitford P. Allgood's first poetry reading would be, well, unsisterly.

Janine looks at me as if I'm *her* bratty little sister, not Whit's. "Were you eavesdropping on us?"

"What'd you expect? I'm a Resistance spy," I counter, fending off the glares. "And don't you forget it, kids." Whit rolls his eyes. He's clearly woken up on the wrong side of the bed—or floor, as the case may be. Time to change the subject. "So, did you hear about the new mission yet, Bro? It's a toughie."

"I didn't want to tell him." Janine shoots me a look. "He'll want to go. He's in no condition—"

"I'll be the judge of that," Whit interrupts. "You're not my mother."

Ouch. We don't ever talk about Mom and Dad casually anymore.

Janine looks a little hurt, then shakes it off. She smoothes down her cargo pants as she stands up. "Besides, I'm not sure it's one *any* of us should take. The rough intelligence makes it look worse than the mission that got Margo killed."

My nostrils are flaring. "The mission that got Margo killed is exactly why we need to go there, Janine. We should finish what she started."

"Where is it?" asks Whit, struggling to stand up.

"They call it the Acculturation Facility," Janine explains as she crouches down to help him. "They say it's a school, not a prison, but…it's actually worse. It looks like some kind of labor camp. Nothing but young kids."

"How many are there?"

"Almost a hundred," she tells us. "But it's the brainwashing that goes on there that I'm concerned about. Instead of finding one hundred captives wanting escape, we're likely to see them turning against us. In fact, the New Order is programming them to do just that."

"We've got to go," I insist.

"Yeah," Whit agrees. "The One is probably expecting us to be licking our wounds right now, not remotely imagining we'll do something bold like this."

He grabs a fresh sweatshirt off a nearby rack and starts to put it on.

Janine's losing her patience. She folds her arms across her chest authoritatively. "Whit, this is a really bad idea."

Her eyes shift to a rack of cycling shorts that suddenly sprouts a head.

Byron!

"I have unfortunate news for all of you," he says smarmily. "Care to hear it?"

"You weren't eavesdropping on us, were you?" I say indignantly.

He laughs. *"I'm a Resistance spy, and don't you forget it,"* he mimics. I roll my eyes.

"Well? We're waiting for your *unfortunate news,*" I say.

"Just because Margo was...*eliminated,*" Byron emphasizes, "it doesn't mean that suddenly Janine is leader of the week. Nor you, Wisty, nor Whit. This mission isn't your decision."

"Then whose is it?"

"Mine," Byron announces with a ridiculous chest heave. "While Whitford's been reciting love poetry and Janine's been nursing Mr. Heroic back to health, you've all missed the majority vote of the group back at Home Furnishings for leader of the week."

He clucks as we stare at him, gaping. "Next time, you might want to make sure you pay more mind to your civic duties."

I guess you can take the kid out of the New Order, but you can't take the New Order out of the kid.

Chapter 18

Wisty

HAVE YOU EVER TRIED to cut off *all* of somebody's hair with a pair of scissors?

It's incredibly hard to do without achieving a certain insane-asylum look. I actually do a pretty good job on Whit—he looks kind of like a war-movie hero. Apparently Emmet's hack job on my head doesn't fall into the same category, though. (I wouldn't let my brother come *near* my hair with scissors.)

"At least you don't have to worry about that witchy red color any longer." Byron cackles as we pull up to the Acculturation Facility. "Except for a couple of patches."

"Who invited you on this mission anyway, B.?" I grumble, even though I know we don't have a choice. He's our way in—but I can't help but fear this is a trap. I can't bring myself to actually trust Byron Swain.

At least Sasha and a few others are with us—but they're back manning the escape vehicles hidden beyond the tree line.

Byron unfurls his folio of various New Order badges and medals and memberships and ID cards at the guards at the entry, and then he drags us, handcuffed, through the door to the registration area.

The whole place has that oh-so-distinctively-generic-New-Ordery blandness to it. If it were a turtleneck color in my K. Krew clothes catalog, it would be called Dirty Dishwater.

"I've got Stephen and Sydney Harmon here," Byron says with an exaggerated bluster of authority. He plays the part so well. Maybe because he *is* the part? "Transfers from AC Facility #625. The One Who Reassigns is expecting them—I just spoke to him an hour or so ago."

"Certainly, Mr. Swain. They're expected. The elevators are down the hall to your left."

Byron's in his element as he theatrically

yanks us this way and that and into the elevators. Once we sink down a couple of levels, he shoves us out the door. "Okay, *Harmons.*" He grins. "You're on your own. See you on the other side."

As much as I sort of hate Byron, I have to admit, getting into an N.O. joint has never been so easy. His timing is perfect—as the elevator doors close behind us, we encounter a group of passing kids and join the rear of the party.

They're heartbreakingly pathetic, these "students." Skinny, hopeless, haunted-looking, and silent as monks. The spirit of youthful anger and rebellion has already been sucked out of them. No complaints, no sarcasm, no anything. They're so beaten down, they don't even seem to notice our arrival.

We follow the procession as it pushes through double doors at the end of the hallway.

At first we're almost blinded by the bright blue-white light bombarding us, but when our eyes adjust we find ourselves in what looks like it might have once been a school auditorium but is now something very different, and sinister.

All the theater seats have been removed, and the large room, including the stage, is now occupied by machines, chemical vats, and dozens of sick-looking kids in numbered shirts, working like diamond-mine slaves. Some of the kids in here are carrying sacks, some are stirring vats, some are pushing around technical equipment.

Our eyes are stinging as if there's something poisonous in the air. The whole place stinks like burning rubber, ozone, and, weirdly— *Could it be?*—chocolate. *Toxic* chocolate. Is there such a thing?

Then there's a weird flutelike note, a middle C if I'm not mistaken, and I look over to see a squad of kids—all wearing the number twelve—suddenly stop working.

And then I see the one adult in the room, a stiff-backed man in a white lab coat with a silver pitch-pipe thingy on a cord dropping out of his mouth.

"Attention squad twelve!" he screams. He waits a moment, and the veins in his neck

slowly subside while his eyes roll. *"Does anyone remember? You may* not—*under any circumstances*—*drop the pods!"*

He blows a different note on the pipe, and they all nod robotically.

"Since these two sacks contain damaged specimens," he says, hoisting a couple of bags over his head, *"you are all hereby required to work through the night without sleep!"*

"Bu—," a sunken-eyed girl starts to say before catching herself.

"But?" screams the man. *"Did you just say 'but' to me?* Need I remind you that the penalty for arguing with a senior scientist requires *level two corporal punishment?"* The man rushes forward to heave the girl—who is probably only a quarter of his size—against the wall.

I want to charge in and sack the guy myself, and I have to reach out and grab Whit's arm to keep him from doing the same. We can't go down in a blaze of glory. Not just yet.

The girl begins to sob, the first glimmer of emotion I've seen in this place so far. A look of small-minded disgust seizes the "senior scientist's" face, and he blows a harsh F-sharp on his whistle.

As if in immediate response, the girl bangs her head against the wall.

He laughs and blows the whistle again. *Bang* goes the girl's head.

Whistle. *Bang.* Whistle. *Bang.* It's sickening, and I can't help myself any longer. I can't hold back.

"Sir!" I yell indignantly. *Oh cripes. Oh crud. Oh kill me now.*

Of course he immediately spins and sends a daggerlike glare across the room. *"You two, come here!"*

Chapter 19

Whit

I LOVE MY SISTER, but she sure doesn't have the, um, *emotional DNA* of a spy. She's 99 percent passion, 1 percent plan. But before I have a chance to step up and fix this situation, the crazed senior scientist starts lurching toward us like a zombie on meth.

"Don't you know getting caught without the proper squad uniform is grounds for solitary confinement? I'll give you *three seconds* to tell me what you're doing here before I set off the alarm and have you *jailed!"*

I pull Wisty forward confidently. *"Sir!* Stephen and Sydney Harmon, reporting to squad twelve for pod duty, *sir!"* I salute him for effect, and Wisty follows my lead.

Suddenly the Lab Boss's popping, pulsing veins soften into a more easygoing throb. "Ah! The famous Harmons! I wasn't expecting you so soon, but I'm delighted you're here."

He turns to his "students." "Squads! The Harmons are triple-A-grade pupils from Facility #625. They're leaders in their category, awarded triple Sector Leader's Stars of Honor, and will serve as role models for all of you. This is good! This is excellent!"

Score! It looks like Byron's intel was good — these Harmon kids were actually being transferred today, but we intercepted their arrival, as planned.

The Lab Boss steps in close to Wisty and me. His breath smells like something I haven't whiffed in ages but that is all too familiar: alcohol. Strictly forbidden by the New Order. "Your first assignment, Harmons, is to supervise the lab for a few minutes. Nature calls, you know!" He laughs inanely. "You of course know how the Command Pipe works, correct?"

"Absolutely, sir," I say, even though Wisty and I don't have a clue.

He presses the whistling instrument into my hands and turns to the rest of the group.

"Squads!" he shouts as if everyone here is deaf. "If productivity doesn't *increase by ten percent* in my absence, you'll *all* be sent to the *Office of Electrical Corrective Punishments!"*

And, leaving us with that happy image of shock treatments and Lord knows what else, he disappears through the lab's double doors.

"Did he just put us in control of this entire lab?" Wisty cocks her head and whispers to me.

"Looks that way. But I'm not sure what that gets us."

"And these kids are all controlled by that pitch pipe?"

"Like border collies, I guess," I say, remembering the headbanging little girl.

"Only it couldn't be *that* easy, could it?"

I look down at the pipe, wipe off the bully's slimy saliva on my sleeve, and blow in it full force like a referee on a basketball court.

The entire roomful of bodies freezes and, almost in slow motion, every single kid collapses to the floor. No, no, no, no, *no. What have I done?*

Chapter 20

Whit

"OH MY GOD, Whit. Are they—? Are they—?" Wisty is suddenly stuttering. I toss her the pitch pipe and run to the nearest fallen boy to check his pulse.

"Alive," I tell her, relief rushing over me. "But we're *all* dead if the Lab Boss comes back now. You've always been the musical one, Wist—you try it. Quick!"

She takes, the pitch pipe and methodically plays a bunch of different scales across the three octaves in the instrument's range. After about a half dozen of them—*Holy frijoles*—every single one of the squad members is looking at us transfixed. But at least they're alive.

"Say something," whispers Wisty. "Give them a command."

"Stand up!" I bellow.

There's not even a pause. We stare dumbfounded as an entire room of kids gets up off the floor—and then starts *bouncing* in place. The weirdest part is...they're all *smiling* as they bounce.

"Wow," I say. It suddenly occurs to me that this is probably the most fun-resembling thing they've done in recent memory. That's my best guess anyway.

Wisty has to blow a couple of dozen notes just to get them to stop. In the process we manage to figure out that one note equals one command.

I'm getting anxious. "Sydney, the boss has just taken the longest wizzer ever, and he's gonna be back in seconds." Spy rule #1: Remain in character at all times. "Let's do this thing!"

My sister quickly plays about six scales and, pointing at me, yells, "Follow this guy!" And I take off out the lab door.

We burst into the hallway, with Wisty bringing up the rear of our sickly white-smocked platoon.

The only problem is that not twenty yards down the hall, coming back from his relief mission, is the Lab Boss.

"Stop, stop all of you! Stop in the name of The One—"

Without missing a beat, I charge forward—it's a Hail Mary move. I deliver a devastating right shoulder to the guy's solar plexus, sending him sprawling onto the institutional linoleum, where, before he can cover himself, he's promptly trampled by twenty-four groups of underage slave lab workers.

My head feels as if it's about to split open from the overpowered alarms that have somehow been set off and are now screaming from every corner. The hall's gone entirely dark except for emergency strobe lights.

As we clamber toward the basement stairwell, I hear boot steps rolling like thunder from above. A legion of them.

From behind me, Wisty's mad pipe-playing music tumbles frantically like the soundtrack of some silent horror movie from long ago. *What is she doing?*

"This way!" yells a voice from down the hall, away from the stairwell. *Byron?*

I turn and lead the kids toward his voice, praying he's still on his best behavior. The kids are actually pretty fast, maybe because they're used to moving quickly to get their chores done and avoid swinging billy clubs.

But they're not faster than the New Order's steroid-fed adult guards. The big jackbooted bullies are only about twenty yards away now. Fifteen? Ten?

Zzzziiiiiiick-ping! A stun-gun wire zips past my head and hits the metal railing next to my hand.

Byron's directing the kids through an alternate passageway, presumably to an underground exit. And Wisty's still playing like a freaking pied piper.

In the flashes of the strobe light, I catch sight of something surreal over my shoulder. Soldiers slowing down, swirling around Wisty...entranced...by the music?

We're going to make it, I think, just as six stun-gun bolts hit me in the back.

Chapter 21

"THAT'S HER," mutters The One with a mixture of hatred and grudging respect. The security cameras in Acculturation Facility No. 73 had recorded the bizarre scene of guards—New Order elites, no less!—being subdued by, of all things, a mere three-octave Command Pipe. She was the only one who could have that kind of power....

The picture is quite dark and he can barely make out what is going on in the flashes of the alarm lights, but he is certain that Wisteria Allgood is the perpetrator of this crime. But how could she—and, presumably, her insipid brother—have gotten into the school? *They're just stupid teenagers.*

The One remembers the last time he lost her, in the plaza, then the mad chase through the city. She and her brother were Curves. They could travel through portals. Was it therefore possible that...?

"Bring me The One Who Commands The Portal Troops, *now!*" he yells.

A moment later a young man with carefully combed hair, an absurd-looking goatee, and a chin so weak it might be confused for his Adam's apple is escorted into the room by two burly guards. He wears a military uniform with a metallic N.O.P.E. insignia on his left breast—marking him as an official in the New Order Portal Elites, a squad of special commandos whose members are among the rare few Curves allowed in the New Order.

"Commander," says The One Who Is The One, "can you please tell me why I was not informed that there was a portal leading into the basement of the Acculturation Facility?"

"Your Eminence," he says, "there is no portal in the facility. It has a clean bill of health."

The One snorts so loudly that the portal

commander actually jumps. "What you just said, those words you uttered with such confidence and aplomb, mean nothing to me. If I tell you there is a portal there, there *is* a portal there! Do you understand?"

"Well, Your Eminence, the entire facility was just inspected—less than a week ago."

"We have recorded evidence of small portals forming in a matter of twenty-four hours or less. It must be a new portal. *Now* do you understand?"

The commander shifts uncomfortably. "Indeed, sir." He clears his throat. "Have you—ah—considered the possibility of magic, sir?" He chuckles nervously, realizing the word is, of course, banned, except among the highest circles—or in certain emergencies, such as this one.

"Do you think that's *funny?*" demands The One. His voice is so cool and restrained it sends wave upon wave of shivers up the portal commander's spine.

The One turns away and watches as the security footage replays itself, grimacing as the witch hastily climbs over a carpet of—dead?

slumbering?—soldiers, then disappears into darkness.

"She is definitely the one with The Gift," he mutters.

"Excuse me?" asks the portal commander.

"I need you to tell me where that portal leads. And I need you to dispatch your best commandos to go through it and infiltrate the Resistance fighters. *Now!* Don't fail me."

Chapter 22

Wisty

I CAN'T BEGIN to tell you how fantastic it is when we return to Garfunkel's—and a hero's welcome. Mr. Homecoming King Whit Allgood is, of course, used to it from his old life. But truants like me rarely get the crowds cheering.

Janine hurls herself at Whit and he doesn't seem to mind, obligingly wrapping his arms around her.

Meanwhile Emmet surprises me with a bear hug and holds on to me just a little longer than I would have expected him to. Maybe as if... he'd been a little *worried* about me?

He interrupts my pathetic little fantasy by

rubbing his hands all over my creepy-looking head. "Bald is beautiful, baby!" He laughs.

I blush, but I'm elated. I'm so high that I can't even feel annoyed that Byron's getting lifted up on the shoulders of shaved-headed kids like a war hero. I let it slide. We couldn't have done it without him, I guess.

Byron howls idiotically—clearly on a head rush from "feeling the love" for the first time in his sad life, poor little weasel—and finally lets himself fall backward. The roaring crowd starts passing him above their heads as if we're in a throbbing mosh pit. It's madness. But it's totally great to celebrate something for a change. I'm soaking in the smiles rather than the usual tears and long faces.

Sasha knocks into me, and I grin at him. "If the weasel gets over here, I'm letting him drop," I say, staying in character. Eternally ungrateful Wisty.

Sasha ignores it. "You look very punk rock!" he shouts. "I like it. It suits you."

"And you look like a bucket of frozen lizard pus." I'm still grinning.

"I'm not kidding. You look totally hard-core. Maybe we could use you at the underground concert."

"What concert?" Someone bashes into me, and I'm almost thrown off balance. "Don't we have more important things on our plate?" I ask, though I admit I'm intrigued.

"This concert *is* important. It's a great opportunity to get new recruits to the cause. Trust me. Maybe even get some intelligence about what other Resistance units know. As a bonus, the concert breaks all their precious rules!"

God knows I'd love to hear some real music. Almost everything's been banned by the New Order for some moronic reason. Causes too much "disorder," I guess. And joy.

Suddenly I'm starving for music, and it's as if Sasha can read my mind. He pulls me away from the mosh pit and takes out his guitar from underneath one of the makeup counters.

"I've been rehearsing." He starts picking out a riff, and I smile—I know the song. It's been a lifetime since I've heard it, but chills run up my spine.

I jump in, singing right on the first line, and Sasha cuts off. "You know it?"

"Are you kidding? I live and *breathe* that song. Give me the guitar."

Sasha hands it over, looking bemused. But with the first chord I strum, I feel as if a switch inside me has been thrown into the *on* position—as if power is literally coursing through my body—and suddenly, even though the guitar's not plugged into anything, it sounds as if I'm hooked up to a sweet amplifier stack.

I take a few steps up the immobile escalator so I can survey the crowd below, and I belt out the famous song's first few lines. I close my eyes as I feel the lyrics swell up inside me and pour out with this crazy mix of joy and pain. I can't stop myself, and I sing this great tune that we all grew up with. It's called "Born to Fly," written and sung by Luce Winterstein, one of my faves.

And, as I sing the final chorus and open my eyes, I see the entire population of Garfunkel's looking up at me, Wisteria Allgood, and they're cheering, hooting, applauding. Meanwhile, Byron is still moshing—or being moshed?—down below.

I realize with a shock that the sound—that glorious blare of music that's so loud it's rattling my bones—isn't just in my mind. It's real! There's a wall of amplifiers that I apparently have conjured up *out of thin air.*

I strum the last power chord, hold it, and tack on a final "Oh yeah!"

Well, I guess I've got my mojo back anyway.

Chapter 23

Wisty

EVERYTHING ABOUT THIS IS forbidden, *banned,* and maybe that's why it's so incredibly great. One step into the Stockwood Music Festival, and it feels as if you've been transported out of the New Order nightmare and into a dream of a place owned by us, ruled by us, and pumping with the fresh blood of music, very good music, astonishing music that just makes you want to dance—which is also forbidden.

"I don't know what Whit was thinking, passing up the opportunity to come here," I say to Janine, who's walking behind me, both of us bouncing on the balls of our feet. My brother had—characteristically—insisted on staying behind to protect the younger kids who needed to remain at Garfunkel's. And he had—uncharacteristically—mumbled some blah-blah about "having a feeling" something bad might happen if there was a "power vacuum" there.

But this... *this* was a once-in-a-New-Order-time experience. "I'm gonna kick Whit's tight little butt when we get back," I finish.

Janine blushes at the mention of Whit's butt. The girl's all brains and heart—but when you mention anything about bodies, she gets embarrassed. "Yeah," she says, and gets all therapist on me. "He needs this more than any of us."

The concert's being held in what was once the underground reservoir for a small village called Stockwood. It's been totally drained and is now just a stadium-size cavern, illuminated by portable road-crew lights. I feel as if I'm on a movie set, because I'm seeing people milling around in dress ranging from medieval monks' robes and ninja outfits to white face paint and black capes.

No wonder creativity's been banned. It's

way too freaking cool for the New Order to handle.

"I didn't realize there was a come-as-your-favorite-comic-book-hero theme," I remark to Sasha and Emmet.

"Not exactly," says Sasha. "They've come here in costume to honor characters from the banned movies and books that they used to love."

"Love," I say. "Present tense." I won't let the N.O. take that away.

"Absolutely," drawls Emmet. "This is all an empowerment kinda thang."

I see exactly what he means. There's banners and handheld signs with slogans like N.O. CAN'T DO and NOTE TO N.O.: WE WILL ROCK YOU.

Just then there's a huge tremor, and little bits of dust and debris curtain down from the ceiling. I have a moment of panic, my head instinctively swiveling around, half expecting to see soldiers pouring in to terrorize us.

Everybody chills, but there are no aftershocks, and moments later we're back to communing, chanting, and proselytizing for the

Resistance. It's as if nothing had happened. A New Order bomb must have landed directly overhead. No biggie. Just another thorn in our sides.

Speaking of which, Weasel Boy comes bobbing up to us. "Hey, guys!" The smug look on Byron's face makes me want to ralph. "I acquired some backstage passes for us! Party *on!*"

Party on? I guess all of the times I've told him to stop talking like such a blowhard have paid off, but I'm not sure I love the result.

"Not interest—," I start to say, but Janine cuts me off.

"You got *backstage passes?* You mean we'll get to meet the *Bionics?*" screams Janine as if she's the world's original teenybopper. Weird—I didn't think she had an ounce of teeny to bop in her. She lifts Byron right off the ground with a hug. *Man, these Bionics must be really good.*

"I thought this was supposed to be an open-mike thing," I say.

"It is," says Byron as Janine lets go of him. "But they're doing it for free. Why are you asking? Were *you* going to get up on the stage?"

"Maybe I was."

I start to blush, until Byron replies unctuously, "Well, I'll get you on the list. Consider it done."

"Forget it," I say. I can't give Byron the satisfaction. "Not interested. Let it go."

"Come on, Wisty," says Janine. "You were good back at Garfunkel's."

Just then another bomb crashes overhead, and dirt rains down from the ceiling. Byron doesn't even flinch. He just turns and stalks off toward the stage.

Janine, Emmet, and Sasha chatter with excitement. Meanwhile, I'm standing here thinking, *Gee, isn't it rather inconvenient to be in the middle of an underground cavern in the middle of a war? Where tons of rocks could come tumbling down and bury us alive at any minute?*

None of that dispels the incredible energy of the concert scene, though. Onstage right now is a group that uses only their mouths to create the music of a full band. Some of them sound like guitars, some like basses, some like drums, some like trumpets, some like instruments that haven't yet been invented.

Janine is giggling and pointing at the stage. It's as if just being here is changing her whole demeanor. She's being...a normal person.

Next we watch these young guys who do incredible balletic duels. Leaping, spinning, twisting, and defying gravity.

And then there's a mind-blowing dance troupe that does their entire show on stilts. It just keeps going....

If there's one thing that makes me hope we stand a chance against the New Order, it's the knowledge that we have so much talent.

Talent — and *passion.*

That's what scares the N.O. about us, isn't it? We've got it, and they don't. We all have the gift.

Chapter 24

Whit

WHAT HAVE I DONE?

I'm sitting on the roof of Garfunkel's bombed-out, dilapidated department store, looking down at the journal in my lap. How could I have ever put such a thing down on paper, much less thought it up in the first place?

This poem I've just written wasn't plagiarized from Lady Myron or anyone else. I have to take full responsibility for these sickening words.

I look off at the horizon, past the outskirts of this burned-out city and the yellowing hills. I see a lazy squadron of bombers passing along, their contrails turning pink in the light of the setting sun. Is it that the world's turned upside down? That everything that was normal yesterday is extinct today? Or is this whole Celia thing just slowly driving me crazy, turning me into some death-obsessed poet?

Just then I hear voices.

I run to the edge of the roof and look down at the bomb-pocked street. A small gang of slacker-looking dudes in black T-shirts and jeans is laughing and walking toward the building's entrance. I have no idea who they are, but at least we know nobody employed by the New Order wears black jeans and Ts. Or has long hair.

Still, I have a bad feeling. Just like the one I'd told Wisty about, before she and the rest left for Stockwood.

I zip down the fire escape to see what's going on with these guys.

Turns out they're a band looking for the Stockwood Festival. Why a bunch of musicians wouldn't know the whereabouts of the biggest concert ever in Freeland seems a little suspicious.

Also suspicious is that they radiate jerkosity.

They keep snickering and slapping each other on the back, saying things like "Righteous" and "Big-time," the kinds of expressions used by guidance counselors who are trying a little too hard.

The leader—a guy with too much gel in his hair and this horrible wannabe goatee—looks me up and down. "Are you the man here?" he asks.

"Nobody's really the leader here. And nobody else is here anyway."

"They at the music festival?" he asks.

"I think it's something like that."

"You have directions? Like I said, we're a band. We're called the Nopes. Ever heard of us?"

I resist the obvious response and just shrug my shoulders. "I think it's in a stadium in the next city, down the old interstate—about twenty miles south of here."

"Really? I heard it was north, dude. The *other* way."

"That's what they told me anyhow," I say. "I honestly don't know. Sorry, guys."

"Well, we'll come back here if you got it

wrong," he says with a threat in his voice. "Hey, can you tell me this: will Wisteria Allgood be there? At Stockwood?"

"Wist-a-who?" I say, hoping I don't look panicked. Even though I kind of am.

"Wisteria Allgood, the Youth Resistance leader," he repeats.

"I think I've heard of her," I say. This is getting worse and worse — the "Youth" Resistance is something you just don't hear us referring to ourselves as.

I shiver and look back casually at the visitors. "Hey, guys, it's getting late, and I'm supposed to go meet some friends for a pickup game. Want to come?"

"We're musicians, not jocks," he says, narrowing his eyes at me. "Come on, guys. We better get rolling so we can do some rocking."

And, with that line — a dead giveaway that they *aren't* "rockers" — they turn and walk away. I watch until they round the corner.

As soon as I'm pretty sure the phonies in black are gone, I take the fire-escape stairs three at a time. Up in my makeshift room, I flip open my journal to take another look at the poem I'd written earlier. And, as if by some otherworldly magic, I see a short message instead.

It packs quite a punch.

GO TO YOUR SISTER. SHE NEEDS YOU. TRUST NO STRANGERS.

It's written in familiar handwriting. Like *my father's* handwriting.

And then, when I blink, it's gone.

I flip madly through the journal, hoping to find it again to convince myself I hadn't hallucinated, but instead I come across my most recent poem.

Another wave of panic comes over me.

What on earth made me write a six-page poem about the *death of my sister?*

Chapter 25

Wisty

I HAVE TO ADMIT, I nearly lose my nerve, just watching the level of talent that's been assembled onstage. I also know that this crowd can be brutal if they don't like your music.

Worse, I almost say thank you to Byron for getting us passes so that we can watch the acts from back here. We're so close we can see droplets of sweat, and the way a singer's mouth forms around a particular word, and the speed of a guitarist's fingers.

And then the Bionics are up.

Okay, *now* I understand Janine's personality switcheroo. They're by far the hottest band *ever*. How do I know? Because seeing their sweat is actually a turn-*on* and not a turnoff.

That has never happened to me before. Sweat usually equals stinky Whit-hug after a track meet.

Everything is different with these musicians. It's as if they're on a whole other plane from everybody else. The singer-bassist, the guitarist, and the drummer—who I consider the cutest of the three (though it's not like I'd say no if any of them asked me out)—brush by me on their way to the stage. I can practically taste their rock-star auras, their *magic*.

They take up their instruments as the hunky lead singer says a generous and humble thank you to the adoring crowd—and I find myself actually squealing with Janine. No wonder the Bionics are banned by the N.O.

But then—*What the heck? How could—?*

Suddenly an enormous poster of The One Who Is The One is rising up behind the band.

I know it's just a poster, but I'm totally creeped out, seeing him looming over the stage like that.

The audience hushes, too. Just a picture of that evil monster is enough to throw a pall over the concert hall.

But then—totally brilliant—the band strikes the first chord of their first song, and the poster catches fire in the lower-left corner. The whole thing quickly goes up in flames as the underground arena explodes in the most unbelievable screams and cheers.

I don't know how to explain it—I mean, I know I can't do what they do, but I'm not intimidated; I'm *inspired.*

And it's a good thing, too, because their set—eight great songs—seems to go by in a flash. And then it's just like the open-mike list says—next up is a little-known wonder hailing from...Garfunkel's department store?

"*Wisteria Rose Allgood!* Give it up for her!"

The Bionics drummer actually winks at me as he walks by. And, at least in part to keep my face from exploding into a fierce blush, I dash out onto the stage.

Chapter 26

Wisty

"UMM, HI, EVERYBODY," I manage to say after a few seconds in which I feel totally flash-frozen. What did I just get myself into?

The brilliant spotlights and—even more blinding—the glare of hundreds, make that thousands, of pairs of eyes...looking right at me.

This is definitely a little more than I was expecting or prepared for. It's definitely a little frightening...but it's also exhilarating. I feel a strange connection to all these people. We're in this together, right? It's us against the big bad N.O. They've got the guns, but we've got the numbers.

"How 'bout those Bionics, huh?" I ask lamely, but they reward me with a massive cheer anyway. Cool. I guess they're in a generous mood.

"So I'm going to sing a couple of songs," I say, trying to slow my speech down and not blurt or stutter. "But first I just want to remind you all of one important thing. You know how we're kind of outnumbered outside of Freeland?"

Massive *boo.*

"And you know how they've taken away so many of us? Just kids, even little babies. They have control of the cities. They have the country. They have the planes. They have the tanks."

Right then, almost as if on cue, the chasm shakes and shudders from another overhead bomb blast.

More massive boos.

"But what they don't have is our spirit. That...they *cannot* have!"

Massive cheers.

"And not only that but—as a kid I met

in one of their horrible prisons reminded me — *they're afraid of us.* That's why they're hunting us. That's why they stage their plots and propaganda against us. That's why they bomb —"

There's another ground-shaking blast from the surface.

"— the world like there's no tomorrow. It's because, for them, there *is* no tomorrow. No next generation. No *future,*" I continue. "And we're not going to give it to them either! Not now, not ever!"

Massive cheers that last for minutes. This is maybe the best thing that's ever happened to me.

"There's just one other thing," I say when my voice can be heard again. Then I produce my drumstick, the one my mom gave me the night Whit and I were kidnapped. "They don't have our ... *magic!*"

And, with that, I grab a guitar and even more lights come up, revealing that I'm standing in front of a newly conjured amp stack that nearly reaches to the ceiling. Now I'll be even louder than the Bionics.

I strike the first chord of my first song, and I've never felt so amazing, so blessed, in my entire life.

At least until Byron comes onstage with a bass guitar and joins in.

Chapter 27

Wisty

EVEN WITH THE KING of the Weasels in my band, I totally understand why people want to become rock stars. There's no other rush, no other feeling like it. This cavern has a natural reverb that seems to transform my voice into a chorus of hard-rocking angels. It's like an out-of-body experience.

And then I realize I'm playing the audience, too. Hundreds, make that thousands, of people are moving to my rhythm, to my melody, to my words.

Well, not *all* "my" words.

After I finish the first song and I think my face is going to bust open because I'm smiling so hard from the euphoria, I let everyone know who wrote the words to the next number.

"This is for my brother, Whit, who wrote the lyrics and who unfortunately couldn't be here with us tonight."

I'm actually pretty glad Whit's not here, because I'd have to explain how I kind of copied the lyrics out of his journal when he was sleeping. I don't regret it, not for a second. I've wanted to put these words to music ever since I first read them.

"It's called 'The Fire Outside,' and it goes like this." I begin picking out a simple, clean melody.

Byron waits a few bars and sticks a bass line underneath. We are disturbingly in sync, I have to admit. Musically, I mean. Apparently he must have been a pretty good upright bass player in the school orchestra back home, and he's showing a surprising sense of rhythm here. With his shirt untucked and his hair kind of messy for once, he almost looks like he belongs at a rock concert.

Lighters are being held aloft, and a whole

cavern full of people is swaying back and forth to the music we're making.

No sooner are Byron and I laying down the final chords when the six-foot-one poet himself appears at the back of the amphitheater. *There he is!* Whit is peering around intently, his head bobbing, as if he's trying to find somebody, and it's important.

Now he's sidling through the crowd toward the stage. He's shooting urgent looks at me and drawing his finger across his neck as a sign for me to stop the set, and pointing off to the dressing-room area to the left.

Something's definitely up.

Chapter 28

Wisty

THE POWER OF THE STAGE and the crowd is too much to resist, though. I finish the song first. Whit deserves to hear his words sung out to the masses.

Then I hurry backstage, expecting him to accost me—or strangle me?—instantly, but...*he's MIA.*

"You were fantastic out there," says Byron while I look around for Whit. "If this magic thing doesn't work out, you could always be a musician, you know. I mean, I guess after you failed out of orchestra in, what was it—fifth grade?—I just assumed you were hopelessly terrible."

"Yeah, well. It took you long enough to

realize that a perfect grade point average isn't the only measure of somebody."

"Definitely *not*," says Byron. He steps toward me with an infuriating eager-beaver expression on his pinched little face. "I really should have taken you seriously a lot sooner, Wisty. I want to make up for that."

Ew. He's not doing what I think he's doing, is he? Please, somebody tell me Byron Hall Monitor Swain is *not trying to put his weaselly moves on me.* I don't want to hurt his feelings, especially tonight, but he's not leaving me much choice.

"I was wrong to underestimate you," he goes on, inching even closer—and there aren't many inches left at this point. "I mean, you were always beautiful, anybody could see that, but I guess I never appreciated...the brains behind your...badness." He said "badness" with a sly smile, as if he were thinking about a kind of badness...of which I wanted *no* part. *Gross!*

"You know, Byron, maybe it's just exhaustion from the show, but I just threw up in my mouth a little bit. You might want to back up."

"Oh, here, let me give you a hand," he says, and puts one of his ferrety paws on my arm. Next, he's steering me toward the "greenroom" couch made out of nongreen cushions pilfered from furniture in bombed-out homes.

I'm so shocked that Byron Belly-Crawler Swain has his hands on me that I can't even react. I should have shoved him off the stage when I had the chance.

"I know some great massage techniques for all sorts of exhaustion," he's saying, but just then the Bionics and a swarm of their groupies burst into the room... along with my brother.

I guess the universe hasn't totally forsaken me.

Chapter 29

Whit

"WHAT'S GOING ON?" Wisty asks me as she pivots away from Byron's pathetic clutches. Normally I'd be ready to teach him a lesson for putting his creepy claws on my sister, but now I'm just relieved to see that he's not one of the fake rockers who were nosing around at Garfunkel's.

I'm pretty sure they're here somewhere— and they're definitely looking for my sister. It's becoming increasingly clear to me that she has something that they want. Badly.

"New Order spies," I tell her. "And they're after *you*, Wist. So next time you decide to take the stage at a packed concert, will you give me a heads-up? You know, so I can tell you that it's a totally boneheaded idea."

"Huh? What spies?" she asks, looking only mildly distressed. Meanwhile her eyes are darting over to some of the rock-star types being swamped by chirping groupies and whatnot on the other side of the room.

"Wisty, listen to me. Closely. Some guys came by Garfunkel's asking after you and the concert. They were dressed like some old person's idea of a rock band. They were obviously New Order Citizen Patrol, or worse."

Her head drifts off toward the fan herd again, so I put my hands on either side of her face and swivel it back toward me.

"Oh, okay." My sister blinks several times, finally processing what I'm saying. "Are they here? Should I be worried?"

"I gave them the wrong directions, but I don't think I fooled them. We'd better get out of here." I grab her hand, but she shakes me off.

"Whit, I'm okay! This is probably the safest place in the city. We're surrounded by, like, a jillion Freelanders hopped-up on New Order hate. Not to mention half of them are packing weapons—"

"Plastic weapons," I remind her, frowning. "They're in *costume,* for God's sake."

Wisty shrugs. "Costumes, whatever, doesn't matter. We're practically indestructible down here. Can't you feel it? It's the most amazing thing." Her eyes are still glazed over with some sort of euphoria I don't understand. I have a future flash: Wisty, rock star, being interviewed twenty-five years after her career goes south. *They slipped something into my drink that night,* she insists. *I didn't know it. But after that, I was an addict.*

I'm shaking my sister now, and her head swings like that of a bobblehead doll. "Wisty, snap out of it! I know you don't believe me, but I've got this feeling we're on the verge of something *really bad* happening."

"You mean something bad *'like a rabid mad dog, poisoning me,'*" sings Byron, inserting his unwelcome presence as usual, *"'while the fire inside me glows, the fire outside you grows.'"*

Holy freaking crap, what did the weasel just say? Those are *my* words. From *my* journal.

"What the—?" My eyes feel as if they're going to pop out of my head. "You were reading my *journal,* you jerk?"

I can't help it—I grab him by the neck. I've had just about enough of our so-called leader of the week.

Wisty finally comes out of her haze. "Whit!" she shouts, trying to pull me off Byron. It's the first time ever that *she* defends *him!* Didn't I tell you the world's turned upside down? "Byron only knows those words from the song *I just sung.* Up on the stage."

Huh? I don't know how I couldn't have heard the lyrics on my way in. I was so focused on making sure she was safe. Wait a minute...

Wisty was reading my journal? WTH?

I release Byron but give him an extra shove for good measure. I look at Wisty, hoping I heard her wrong. "That's what you were singing up there? Words from my journal?"

"You weren't even *listening?*" she says, then

softens her voice. "It was a tribute to your genius, Whit. I love what you wrote."

Wisty reaches for me, but I'm already stomping out of the room. "You two deserve each other!" I yell back at her and the traitor.

Chapter 30

Wisty

I'M ALMOST READY to follow Whit when my whole body is kind of stun-gunned by this amazing voice behind me.

"So where'd you get the drumstick? It's an antique, right? Classic."

I turn and find I am looking eye-to-mesmerizing-eye with none other than the drummer of the Bionics.

He is talking to me. *The Bionics drummer is talking to me.*

I'm concerned about Whit, really I am, but...he'll get over it, right?

Drummer Boy is even better-looking up close than he was behind his drum kit. If that's possible. He's tucking his overlong, wavy black hair behind his ears, but then it falls right back in his face again. Sweet. I watch his lusciously thick lips move, but I have no idea what he's saying, of course. I don't think I could hear a car crash over my own heartbeat right now. Dumb? Maybe. Fun? Definitely.

"Uh—what?" I finally manage to get out a couple of syllables. I'm unable to meet his hazel eyes for too long, so I find myself staring at his faded black T-shirt, which reads, NO ORDER. I like it. We have something in common already.

"Your drumstick. Kind of funny for a guitarist and a singer to be carrying a drumstick around." He has a nice smile, too. Not too much, just right.

"Yeah, I know." I smile back. Maybe a little too toothily. "My mom gave it to me. I think it's for good luck. It's kind of a collector's item."

"It looks like it," he says. "So your *mom's* a drummer?"

I am not about to ruin this with a mood-killing "I think my mom was a witch and this

132

is a wand she gave me the night I was kid-napped" dud.

"She was," I lie. Ouch. Mom wouldn't like the past tense. "I mean, *is*." That feels even worse. "I mean, *was*." My face goes from pale pink to fuchsia in about three seconds.

But Drummer Boy looks at me with... sympathy? "I know, it's hard." How could he have possibly grasped my blah-blah? "A lot of us don't know if our folks 'is' or 'was.'" He puts a comforting hand on my arm, and my stomach kind of flips. *God, he's sweet. He understands!*

His eyes drift back to my stick. "Can I see it? Is that all right with you?"

"Um... sure!" I start to hand it to him, but as he grabs the end to take it from me, he jumps back, yelping in pain.

"It burned me!" he says, sticking the side of his hand into his mouth. "What's with that?"

"Jeez! I'm so sorry!" I say. I look down at the stick in my hand. It doesn't feel even slightly warm, but it *is* glowing red at the tip where he tried to touch it.

"I had no idea it could do that," I say. "I *really* didn't mean—"

"Don't worry about it," he says, shaking his hand and smiling through the pain. "It's nothing. Especially next to what's happening every day to kids in New Order 'schools,' right?"

"Have you been to one?" I ask, a little surprised.

"Not yet. A little too risky for us. But we've had fan tips about that last facility you raided."

"Er...how do you know about that?"

"You and Whit and Byron made the underground newswire," he says, and shrugs. "You're famous. But you don't act like it."

Byron hears his name across the room like he's got supersonic ears and is by my side in half a second.

"They're practically writing folk songs about you already, Wisty," Drummer Boy continues. "That facility you hit is part of a system of exploitation and experimentation. The New Order calls them Juvenile Education and Repatriation complexes. It's just cheap child labor."

"That's really shocking," says Byron. The boy's like a bad cold. You just can't shake him.

"That's not the worst of it," says the drummer, and I realize I don't even know his name. "There's another place, the BNW Center — the Brave New World Center. We've heard they're doing live human experiments on everybody they keep there. 'Special' kids" — he uses air quotes — "like you and your brother."

Everybody's quiet for a moment, and as the gravity of this sinks in, I lower my eyes from his. "I better go meet up with my brother. He needs to hear about this."

"Yes," says Byron Officious Swain as if he's my aide-de-camp — or, worse, my boyfriend. "Keep us apprised," he tells the drummer. Then he actually grabs my hand and starts pulling me toward the door.

How is it that I mess up with just about the hottest guy I've ever seen — and then find myself holding hands with Byron?

This isn't about being "special"; it's about being *cursed*.

Chapter 31

Wisty

CURSED, YES, but not for long apparently.

That's because Eric—as he finally introduced himself—and the rest of the Bionics decide they want to come back with us to Garfunkel's.

Whit is less than enthused. I have the sense he doesn't trust them—and, of course, he's still mad about the whole stealing-his-journal incident—but with Sasha, Emmet, Janine, and me backing the Bionics, he can't quite say no.

A bunch of us are in the middle of doing an impromptu a cappella version of "The Fire Outside" when suddenly Whit floors the gas pedal while making a sharp turn. Eric's hand *just happens* to slide off his knee and come to rest on my hand. It stays right there. I have no urgent need to remove it.

"Buckle up, everybody!" Whit shouts. "We've got New Order police on our tail."

"Police?" I say, incredulous. "What are they doing here in Freeland?"

"Yeah!" shouts my brother. "And how did they manage to find us is another good question. Now brace yourselves!"

The van accelerates, and I scramble to look out the back windows. Three heavily armed New Order police vehicles are bearing down on us. This looks bad. Whit takes a sharp left turn that sends us all sprawling against the side of the van.

My head's flung against Eric's chest. Talk about making the best of a bad situation.

"Sorry," I mumble.

"S'okay," Eric whispers.

But then a sharp *right* turn sends us rolling violently against the other side.

And now I'm tangled up with Byron. *Ick.*

"They've got us boxed in. Coming from all sides!" yells Whit, braking the van to a rocking standstill. "We'll have to run! Everybody take off in different directions. Hopefully they won't get all of us!"

"No!" I yell. "That's not the best plan. Seriously, just stay in the van!"

Everyone looks at me like I'm crazy, which I might be. We'll know soon enough.

"You guys know the song 'Magic Truck' by the How?" I ask.

Eric starts laying down a beat on the floor of the van. The bassist and guitarist grab their instruments.

Meanwhile, police cars are skidding to a stop all around us—and then a voice is coming over their PA: *"Exit the vehicle immediately and lie on the ground."*

I wave for the band to keep playing. The lead singer starts in, and then I join him. The groove is instant, almost as if we've been rehearsing together for a couple of months.

I hear the policemen pounding on the windows. We answer by turning up the volume.

Then we don't hear the policemen anymore. That's because we've succeeded in levitating the van several hundred feet in the air.

Yeah, you heard me right.

The music was magic. The music did it. The van is still rising in the air.

I look out the back at the police vehicles, and one of the cops is throwing his hat on the ground in frustration.

"That was close. Too close," comments Byron, seeing the glass as half empty.

"It…freaking…*worked!*" I scream, and then I can't help myself—I throw my arms around Eric. *My* glass is very, *very* full.

This is definitely the best night of my life on the *Wanted Dead or Alive* list.

Chapter 32

Wisty

I THINK kissing was involved — I'm not certain, but I'm pretty sure. I think Eric's a good kisser. Not sure, though. The entire evening was kind of a blur....

I wake up inside Garfunkel's the next morning, and I have two distinct thoughts: First: *Did I dream of falling asleep in the drummer's arms, or did it really happen?* Second: *My drumstick is gone!*

It's the first thing I reach out to touch in the morning. And it's not there.

Problem. Big problem. Disaster. That drumstick is my magic wand *and* it's a family heirloom.

Everyone else is deeply conked out after our

night of revelry—so I begin a mad hunt to find the wand my mother gave me just before I was separated from her and dragged off to prison.

I always sleep with the drumstick under my pillow. Or whatever the circumstances are forcing me to use instead of a pillow. But it's not there. And it's not under the mattress either. And it's not in my coat. And it's not in my knapsack. It's *nowhere*.

Okay, don't cry about this. Think, Wisteria. What was different about last night compared to every other night you've slept at Garfunkel's?

Well, the Bionics were here....

That's got to be it—the drummer! Was Whit right about them?

I tiptoe over to Byron—snoring like a buffalo—and expertly swipe his supersecret smartphone and text Eric at the number he gave me yesterday.

where R U?

He texts back right away:

had 2 go practice. didn't want 2 wake u
got yr drumstx?
yep
got mine?
used oven mitt...just in case it was still hot
not funny
sorry
u have it? give back!
tots
you STOLE it
borrowed
i want it back NOW
im sorry. meet me
WTH? u bring it 2 me
don't freak. m sorry. meet @ city of
    progress diner — 11 am
fine
yr so cool
whatevs, I type.

But my heart is leapfrogging, and I'm grateful that cell phones don't convey blushes. I'm cool? As of when?

I mean, it was jerky of Eric to take my stick. But he's a rock drummer and he admired it.

And, I mean, I can almost hear my mother's voice telling me he just did it to get my attention. Just the way she told me why geeky Ben Campbell used to pull my hair in first grade.

Now I *do* start crying. I miss my mother so much. She was my best friend. She *is* my best friend.

Chapter 33

Wisty

I DECIDE against finding Whit and telling him where I'm going, even though he's probably going to kill me when I get back. But I don't really have a choice, because guess what my brother would say?

A) Have a great lunch. Could you bring me back some fries?
B) It's windy out there. Be sure to zipper your coat.
C) Fine, I'm coming with you. No arguments, firebrand!

Yeah. If you picked A or B, I'm going to

politely suggest you turn back a few dozen pages and do some rereading.

I need to have my moment alone with Eric. So I sneak around quietly, making myself ready to infiltrate the City of Progress—the New Order's demented model city, the template they mean to apply to the rest of Freeland after they've stamped out anyone who resists their disgusting ideas.

It takes a little bit of disguise to properly blend in (read: skirts and sweaters for girls, no black lipstick or obvious piercings; jackets and ties for boys, and Byron-style hair preferred), but it's doable, and necessary.

And, since my hair hasn't grown back yet, it's a great excuse for me to lift a new hairdo— a cute little brunette bob—from the wig counter inside Garfunkel's.

I tiptoe out the store's front door, and suddenly I feel a vibration under my arm. More precisely, it's coming from the very un-Wisty-like white purse tucked there.

Another text message. I click the phone on.

A text message *in my mother's handwriting.* *WTH...?*

IT'S OK, WISTY. SHE'S AN ALLY. GO WITH HER.

With *who?* Suddenly I feel very un-alone. I hear someone's voice.

"Well, we meet again, my dear!"

I yank my head to the right, and there, leaning on the hood of a long-dead station wagon, one leg crossed over the other, is the little old ninja lady. The one who gave us the map that saved our lives. And now that I'm able to scrutinize her more closely, I realize she's also the woman who almost got me arrested in a diner on my very first trip to the City of Progress. *Mrs. Highsmith!*

"It's okay," the strange little woman says in a high nasal drawl. "Go ahead and SMS or whatever it is you people do with your silly little gadgets. Your mother's not particularly close, but you'll at least see that she's safe."

I quickly type back,

If she's an ally, y'd she try to get us arrested?

My mother's handwriting replies,

SHE PANICKED—SHE THOUGHT YOU MIGHT BE A NEW ORDER SPY. YOU SAW THEM TRY TO ARREST HER. WHY WOULD SHE WANT TO HELP THE NEW ORDER?

K, but how do I know this is u?

HOW WOULD ANYBODY ELSE KNOW THAT BEN CAMPBELL USED TO PULL YOUR PONYTAIL?

OMG, Mom!!!

I type as tears well up.

GO WITH HER QUICKLY, DEAR. GIVE WHIT A KISS FROM US. DAD AND I ARE THINK- ING OF BOTH OF YOU. ALL OF THE TIME. WE LOVE YOU SO MUCH.

Mrs. Highsmith comes up to me with an old-fashioned handkerchief that I numbly ac- cept. It smells like witch hazel.

"You see? Your mother's okay," says Mrs. Highsmith. "Now, please come with me to my apartment—so we don't get the New Order looky-loos all excited about capturing *two* witches on the same day."

Chapter 34

Wisty

SO HOW DO YOU THINK we get to the City of Progress in about ten minutes flat? Broomstick? Portal? If I told you, you wouldn't believe me—and that's saying a lot, given what I've gotten you to believe about our insane lives so far.

Let's just say Mrs. H. has some powers that might, just might, rival The One's. If I didn't have "Mom" telling me she was on my side… I'd have to wonder.

Okay, check this out: Mrs. H.'s apartment is a cluttered, dimly lit place—the heavy curtains are drawn even though it's a sunny morning. There's not an empty shelf, table, or chair. Even the piano top is covered with novels, hardbacks, paperbacks, notebooks, antique tomes. Obviously all *banned*. The walls are chockablock with pictures—some framed, some crudely taped up—and there's even an easel with a half-finished painting of a dragon on it, which I almost trip over. There's barely a path for me to follow her into the kitchen, which smells like some sort of heavily spiced tuna casserole. It must be 120 degrees in here.

"Pardon me while I finish working on this stew," she says, peering over the lip of a giant black barrel sitting on a couple of hot plates in the middle of the kitchen floor. It's enormous and looks like some kind of oil shipping container. She could fit a small horse in that thing. Maybe she has.

Mrs. H. dips a ladle into the soup for a taste. She offers me some, but I shake my head violently. "Needs some more willow bark and sassafras root anyway," she says. "I underestimated how much this broth was going to absorb."

Okay, remind me: *how* did I end up with an old witch stirring potions in a boiling-hot apartment, instead of with Drummer Boy, chatting and eating burgers in a very cool diner?

"Don't think I don't know what you're thinking," she says with a disapproving look. "So I'll get to the point. Here's the deal: as you may have discovered, The One Who Is The One is a complete yenta."

I look at her quizzically. A yenta? Is that good or bad or something in between?

"A yenta is a person who wants to get into everybody else's business. And, what's worse, he wants to put an end to all their business and make it all about his business. *Everything.*" She pauses to take a sip of her brew and makes a face.

"He's basically a conduit for the worst kind of evil. I'm talking stuff that makes a person want to put out her eyes and ears rather than to see or hear it," she continues, wincing and replacing the ladle in the barrel.

"And, unfortunately, he's figured out a way to get himself more power than any other individual in the history—or even the pre-history—of the world."

"So are you here to tell me he can't be

stopped?" I say. "Typical grown-up stuff? Give it a rest? Get real? Stop fighting for nothing?"

She chuckles to herself. "I'll let that slide, because you obviously don't know me. *Yet.* Now, ready to take notes?"

She picks up her ladle and flings the tip toward one side of the room, then another, and then back toward me, spraying me with disgusting bits of her soup in the process. In a flash a pencil and a piece of paper fly into my hands.

"Didn't know I was in school again, but… okay," I say tentatively, wiping the drops of gag-worthy gruel off my face.

"There are two X factors in this entire situation that can give us the edge. Care to guess what they are?"

"Timing and luck?"

"*Positive energy* and *negative energy*. We need to maintain a surplus of the former. And we need to send that sick son of a gun a good dose of the latter. *Capiche?*"

I nod. *Capiche?*

"Now, I'm no fan of that Stockwood Music Festival—too many sweaty young bodies and too much mindless bobbing and weaving for my taste — but I heard last night through the underground newswire that you're apparently *quite* musically talented." I nod again. "Music, my dear, is a more potent force for change than you may think."

"No offense, Mrs. H., but you have *no* idea how powerful it is unless you've performed on a stage in front of thousands. *Plugged in.*" I shiver just thinking about it. I can hardly wait to get my hands on a guitar again.

"How do you know I haven't?" She chuckles, and I realize that this lady has a past I am definitely going to have to find out more about. "I'm talking about a very different kind of power, Wisty. That's why it's banned by the N.O. Didn't you ever wonder why it's forbidden?"

"I *know* why. 'Cause it's fun, and the N.O. is antifun."

Mrs. H. gives me a look that reminds me of my mom — her *Wisty, stop being funny when you know this is serious* look.

"If there is one thing I need to teach you, it's *never underestimate the power of what you or others create.* Music, art, film, writing, all of this"—she waves her hand around the cluttered apartment—"there's tremendous energy here. This is life force. Very important."

"We'd better hide all of this from them, then," I tell her. "You're crazy to keep it here in the City of Progress. Maybe we can bring it to Garfunkel's."

"No. I need it. I can't let it go. I'll let them take me before they take it."

I'm stunned. Die for kids, yeah, but die for...*art?* I'll have to think about that.

She passes me a folded-up square of paper.

"Learn it. Memorize it. Use it to help others. Pass it on. And on, and on."

I open it and see a crudely drawn musical staff with notes. It looks like a pretty simple melody.

"What does it do?"

She points to a battered guitar that looks kind of lost and abandoned in the corner of the pantry. I hadn't even seen it in all the clutter. "That's for you to figure out. So—go figure."

Before I know it, I'm strumming the guitar

and learning how to "beat the blues," as Mrs. H. calls it. It's . . . *amazing* actually.

Now I just need to figure out how to bust up the New Order, get a restraining order against Byron, and placate Whit. Then the world will be back in its proper orbit again.

Closer anyway.

"Exactly right, dearie! Now *taste*," says the ancient lady, stuffing the ladle in my mouth.

Chapter 35

Wisty

'SCUSE ME as I wipe drool from my chin...

Normally, I might just be talking about the fact that I've ordered a cheeseburger with pickles, shoelace fries, and a black-and-white shake. But today I'm double drooling because I'm sitting with Eric, Bionics Drummer Boy. How could his five o'clock shadow at eleven thirty in the morning and deepened undereye circles make him look even *more* gorgeous? But they do. He simply defies all laws of nature.

We place our orders with the ridiculously efficient waitress who is typical of the help in N.O. eateries.

"Too bad you're not as fast as she is," Eric

quips. "Where the heck were you anyway? I'm, like, on my fifth cup of coffee, here."

"Did you miss me?" I opt to say, instead of *Sorry, but I was busy playing guitar in an old witch's kitchen.*

"Actually yeah," he says. He levels his gaze at me, and I notice a glint of vulnerability in his eyes. "How come you look so crazy beautiful? You couldn't have had much more sleep than me."

Crazy beautiful? Never before has Wisteria Allgood been described as such. Crazy, yes. Beautiful...?

This is *so* nice. I'm *so* not used to the attention.

"Must be the wig," I mumble, and glance down. He's still staring at me. I can feel it. He's reaching across the table...toward my hand...

"Listen, Wisty," he says. His fingers interlock with mine, and the cool metal touch of his insignia ring against my skin is exhilarating. I feel as if my spine has been replaced with an overcooked noodle.

"I'm *really* sorry," he says. I look up at him, and suddenly there's only pain in his eyes now. *Poor thing, taking this drumstick incident so seriously!*

"About the stick? It's nothing—"

I'm interrupted by a commotion at the door, and we both turn to look.

Oh, kill me now. It's my big brother with the savior complex.

"*Wisty, it's a trap!* Get out of there! Now!" Whit yells as a bunch of rock star–looking dudes appear from out of nowhere—and attempt to pin him to the wall.

I try to jump to my feet, but Eric forcefully grabs my wrist.

"I'm so sorry, Wisty," he's whispering. "I had no choice in this."

"What? What *is* this?" I demand to know.

The Bionics singer and guitarist are standing at the opening of the booth now. And they're chewing on unlit cigars.

It can't be. But I'm afraid it is.

"Eric?" I ask, tears starting to spill from my eyes. But Drummer Bum only shrugs and looks away. *Is he doing what I think he's doing?*

How could he have been so wonderful one minute, and now he's turning me over to the New Order?

I'm wrong about people sometimes, but I've never been *this* wrong. I slump forward on the table, feeling as if I've just been stabbed in the chest.

What is wrong with me for walking right into this trap?

I look up into the face of my crush of five minutes ago. I'm searching for a clue, for any of the signs I missed.

But all I see is his near perfect face, and genuine-seeming contrition.

"I had to, Wisty. Don't you see? *You're The One Who Has The Gift.*"

Chapter 36

Whit

BEFORE I CAN REACH Wisty to try to help her escape, somebody hits me hard. Just about all the wind rushes out of me and my knees buckle. I'd probably fall on my face if the three of them weren't so busy trying to pin me to the wall. They're strong—they may look like boys, but they fight like adults. Adult professionals, maybe New Order soldiers.

I only hope I gave Wisty enough warning to help her get out; I only hope I managed to mess up their trap; I only—

Ooomf!

Another smashing blow, this one right to the middle of my face. Stars and bright colors explode everywhere. That couldn't have been a fist. It was too hard.

I'm starting to sink to the ground, but one of these creeps is holding me up and the other is turning my head by the ears, making me look at something.

"See that, Big Brother?" the voice in my ear rings. "Not only did you fail to save your little sister, but we're going to make you *watch* what the Council of Ones does to her!"

My eyes dart down the length of the diner to where Wisty is being dragged out of her booth by the Bionics and one of the soldiers.

And then, suddenly, the Bionics start—I don't know how to describe it—morphing, I guess. They get bigger and older, as if they've aged from seventeen to thirty-five in the space of a few seconds. It's scary—and *gross* beyond anything I can tell you in words.

They're burly, cigar-smoking soldiers now. All of them except one Bionic—the drummer, I think—who's still sitting in the booth, looking like he just accidentally ran over a puppy.

"Do it quickly, you idiots!" yells one of the thugs holding me.

I notice three more soldier-commandos in black flak outfits, each leveling big-bore rifles right at my sister.

"No!" I scream. *"Leave her alone! Don't shoot her!"*

They drop to a knee and pull their triggers almost in unison.

"Wisty!"

And then it's as if time has slowed to a crawl. I watch as the muzzles issue explosions of compressed gas, each propelling a lethal-looking dart at my inhumanly manhandled sister....

Wisty throws one last look at me and I catch it, hold on to it forever. More than anything, I don't want her to die with that desperate look of shame on her face.

I don't want her to die, period.

And then my mind seizes on the hurtling projectiles. Not bullets. Darts. I see the wicked hollow needles on the front of each fluffy-tailed syringe as it bullets toward my sister's torso.

They look big enough to drop a charging

rhino, much less sedate a hundred-pound teenager.

If I just push the first dart's tail a little this way...and this dart a little this way...and this one just like this...

Thwok—

Thwok—

And *thwok!*

The former Bionics and the soldier holding her go wide-eyed as each dart finds its new target...right smack in the middle of each of their necks.

They hit the floor.

Thump.

Thump.

And *THUMP.*

"Unnh!" gasps my sister.

"What's wrong, Wist?" I yell. "What happened?"

My eyes lock on hers, which have gone wide and also a little vacant. And now her lids are fluttering...and she falls face-first right on top of her unconscious attackers.

There's a syringe sticking out of her back, the plunger pushed down.

The drummer!

He's standing behind her. His face is twisted and crumpled with guilt.

"Attaboy!" shouts the soldier who's been holding me. "Now let's get these two reprobates into the paddy wagon and collect our just rewards."

Chapter 37

Whit

THESE GOONS ARE LIGHTING up their victory cigars. Is consigning us to death basically like finishing a steak dinner? Or winning a sports championship? It sure looks like it.

I'm now pinned on the ground, fighting to get my breath back, when a desperate thought pops into my head. Not counting the three guys on the floor with darts in their necks, there are seven cigar-smoking soldiers. There's the drummer, too, but I'm guessing he's just a regular kid. A horrible Tall Jonathan–esque traitor of a kid, but . . . a kid.

I look at each smoldering cigar and, one by one, I visualize the rolled brown tobacco inside. Foul stuff. I hate nicotine poison.

Then I imagine seven capsules filled with a toxic compound a teacher told us about in chemistry. It's called trinitrotoluene. You may have heard of it by its more common name, TNT.

In my mind, I carefully place a capsule inside each of their cigars, about an inch or so from the glowing tip. I wait; I count off the seconds; I hope this will work.

And then, in almost perfect precision —

Blam-blam-blam-blam-blam-blam-blam!

Suddenly there's no more combat boot on my neck. I get to my feet and stumble through the acrid smoke to my sister. I pluck the syringe from her back. Then I throw Wisty over my shoulder.

"Proud of yourself?" I ask the drummer.

He looks at me coolly, and I want to punch him. I satisfy the urge by swiping Wisty's drumstick out of his hand. "They'll kill me," he whispers.

I pause. I don't want the guy to be killed, really. But if I have to choose between my sister and an N.O. puppet, there's no question what to do.

"Tell somebody who cares," I say, then race out of the diner.

But I do care. Sometimes it feels rotten, putting on the face of steely, unwavering courage.

Chapter 38

Whit

THERE'S NOTHING like a three-mile run with your kid sister slung over your shoulder to clear your head. I'll never call her "Wispy" again, that's for sure. She's growing up fast. My back, my lungs, my legs…they all ache so much I want to stop and throw up.

I hear the distant rumble of trucks and the squawks of N.O. loudspeakers. The thumping of a helicopter soon joins the mix—it's coming our way quickly.

I duck off the road and into the woods, hoping the trees will lend some cover.

I find a path through the brush, but I get only about a hundred yards before it forks. The bigger track goes down into a gulley, and the smaller one winds along the side of a hill.

"High road or low road, Wisty?" I say, not expecting her to answer. I prop my sister against a tree. I need to put her down for a few seconds or I'll collapse into a heap.

"There are ants all over this tree," I hear her whisper.

"You're awake!" I'm stunned.

Wisty's already weakly swatting the little black insects off her arm. "Yep. I can even answer your question."

"You mean which road we should take?"

Without missing a beat, she starts murmuring a poem.

Two roads diverged in a yellow wood,
And sorry I could not travel both
And be one traveler, long I stood
And looked down one as far as I could....

I shall be telling this with a sigh
Somewhere ages and ages hence:
Two roads diverged in a wood, and I—

I took the one less traveled by,
And that has made all the difference.

"You wrote that?" I ask, aghast.

"Bertrand Snow actually," Wisty admits.

"Well, you must be winning your battle with the drugs to remember anything from your lit class."

I throw her over my aching shoulder one more time, and just then we hear a vehicle skidding to a stop on the road. Suddenly the woods behind us are alive with heavy-booted footsteps, men yelling...and dogs barking angrily.

"Maybe they'll pick the wrong path," I pant, and reflect that maybe we should have chosen the downward-sloping one. This trail has been 100 percent *up*hill so far.

"Um, I don't think they'll pick the other path, Whit."

"Why not?"

She's craning her neck behind me.

"Um, because I can already see them — *and they can see us!*"

Chapter 39

Whit

I CURSE under my breath and turn to assess. Sure enough, two soldiers and three large German shepherds have crested the last rise in the hill and are charging up the path toward us.

Only, wait—did I say two soldiers and three German shepherds? Because it's actually one soldier and four German shepherds—or, wait, it's *all* German shepherds—

"Did you *see* that?" demands Wisty. "They're turning themselves into dogs! Very *fast* dogs."

"Great," I say, and stop running.

"Why are you stopping?" yells Wisty.

"There's no point. I can't outrun a pack of magical dogs with you on my back. It's simple physics. I'd have to be a horse."

"Well, I've turned myself into a rodent before. Maybe you can turn yourself into a horse. Aim big, Brother. We don't have much of a choice right now."

"I don't know any horse spells—"

"Look in your journal and pray that it's getting good reception today!"

I'm flipping the pages madly, and nothing about a horse catches my eye. It's the first time in my life I actually wish I could look in an *index*.

There's no index, of course, but what I stumble on is even better:

Tyger! Tyger! burning bright
In the forests of the night,
What immortal hand or eye
Could frame thy fearful symmetry?

In what distant deeps or skies
Burnt the fire of thine eyes?

On what wings dare he aspire?
What the hand dare seize the fire?

After I recite the weird poem, the next thing I know I'm on all fours, with black-and-orange-and-white fur, my clothes split up and down and hanging in tatters.

So I turn to ask Wisty the obvious question: *"Rrrrrrooaaarrr?"*

"You're asking if a tiger can kick a bunch of dogs' butts, right?" asks Wisty. "I think so. But let's not experiment if we don't have to, especially with me on your back. Yah, tiger, *mush!*"

And then she digs her heels into my flanks. I yelp, and I take off up the hill—*as a tiger.* Ain't magic great?

The dogs howl in rage behind us, and then there's another noise—another sort of roar? I look back over my striped shoulder and see that our pursuers are now turning themselves into bears, grizzlies actually, as they continue after us.

Who are these guys? And where are they getting their magic?

The answer, unfortunately, reveals itself all too quickly.

We reach the clearing at the crest of the hill and are greeted by a tall bald man in an impeccable dark blue suit. He's standing there as if he's been waiting for us all his life.

Chapter 40

Whit

I WHEEL around immediately. I'd rather face a troop of charging bears than The One Who Is The One. Heck, I'd rather face a lake filled with piranha, a full stampede of tyrannosaurs, a mechanized infantry division...I could go on and on.

But even as we turn away, the trees of the forest weave their yellow-leaved branches and trunks together and seal up the path as if it had never been there. There's no way through, no way out.

The ground buckles and sends us sprawling backward toward the middle of the clearing. Wisty topples off my back and lands with a whimper on the ground.

She's still too messed up by the drugs to stand, but The One doesn't cut her any slack — tree roots shoot out of the ground and quickly smother her in a dirty wickerwork of wooden tendrils.

"Whit!" she screams. "I'm trapped! I can't move!"

There's nothing worse than hearing someone you love scream your name in desperation. Rage boils up inside me. I spin and charge. Five hundred pounds of furious Siberian tiger ready to snap his bald-headed neck like a toothpick, ready to send my sharp teeth into whatever part of him I can reach first.

Unfortunately, The One Who Is The One has other ideas. Suddenly the wind kicks up so fiercely I have to close my eyes. And it's as if I'm a stuffed tiger, flimsy as a carnival prize — and somebody has turned on a giant leaf blower. I'm flipped into the air, and I can't tell up from down. Leaves and dirt are pelting me, stinging me, cutting through even my dense fur, and then — wait! — the wind has stopped already.

For a split second I can see the sky.

And then, oh no—I can see the earth! I make out Wisty's form *so far, far below,* pinned on the hilltop way down there like some human sacrifice. I must be a thousand feet above her.

I hear laughter. *His* laughter…echoing up as if the entire forest is mocking us.

And then I'm no longer a tiger.

I'm just *me* in my torn clothing.

Falling.

Helpless.

He's taken away my mojo, my magic, probably my life.

BOOK TWO

SOMETHING WICKED THIS DAY COMES

Chapter 41

"HAVE A SEAT," says the solemn, tight-lipped man behind the heavy metal desk.

Byron Swain nods nervously and sits on the threadbare couch as the man finishes some official-looking paperwork.

"You took your time getting here," says the stern adult, putting down his overchewed pencil.

"I had to observe all the protocols—"

"No excuses!" yells the man, spraying spittle across the metal desk at Byron. "Children of Ones don't make excuses!"

He again snatches up his battered pencil as if he is going to either break it in two or throw it at Byron's face.

Byron meekly recedes back into the couch, wishing he could somehow slide between the cushions like some accidental pocket change.

"And you will stand up in my presence! Who do you think you are, Byron?"

"I'm sorry, Dad."

"And *stop* calling me that! I am *The One Who Tallies The Internal Revenues.*"

"Yes, sir, I'm sorry, sir," says Byron, remembering how the Freelanders call his father "The One Who Counts The Beans" and making a mental note not to mention that. "I just—"

"Excuses!" he screams. "By order of the New Order, and at the specific request of The One, you will now give me a complete report!"

Byron feels a little pain growing like a cancer in his chest. He isn't happy spying on the Free-landers, but what choice does he have? Wisty continues to reject him. He is nothing to her. To any of them really. And he is under direct orders from his father.

Byron stands at attention and, shaking slightly, begins telling him everything.

Chapter 42

Wisty

TRUST ME, you don't know pain till you know what it feels like to wake up after getting nailed by a New Order tranquilizer dart. Or three. Or twelve.

My eyes ache like they've been loaded on rusty metal springs. My temple throbs like somebody's just nailed a red-hot horseshoe around the inside of it. The back of my head pulses like somebody's trying to inflate it with a bicycle pump.

And my mouth — my tongue feels like it's a slug that's crawled halfway across an equatorial desert and died, and my throat feels like it was just the parade route for a troop of hermit crabs.

And my stomach…sloshing around like I'm in a car with no shock absorbers driven by a drunk who's decided to take a shortcut through a timber yard. "Carsick" doesn't cover it.

"Hey, Wist, how you feelin'?" asks Whit.

I wince and croak back, "What's with all the noise and the bumpety-bump?" I'm still not able to open my eyes properly to see where I am.

"We're having another New Order van ride," he says, helping me sit up.

"Water?" I croak.

Whit shakes his head. "Strangely, they didn't give us the van with the minibar." He leans up toward the front seat. "Anywhere up here on the right will be fine," calls Whit through the grate, as if we're riding in a taxi going to a Sunday matinee. He's trying to cheer me up, I guess.

The goon riding shotgun—and wouldn't you know it, he actually *has* a shotgun—slams the bulletproof-glass divider closed.

"Nice fellow," says Whit. "Maybe a little too intense."

A wave of panic engulfs me now. I don't know if I can go through another imprisonment — the endless hunger, the mind-splitting thirst, the soul-crushing hopelessness....

Whit senses that I'm freaking out. "We'll be okay," he says. "We wouldn't be here today if we weren't survivors, and if we stunk at jailbreaks, right?"

I know he's trying to be sweet, but what an idiotic thing to say. I'd scream at him if my head didn't hurt so much. "We wouldn't be here today if I hadn't fallen for..." *Eric.* I can't even say it. Just the thought of that sad, pitiful, god-awful betrayal is like another knife in my gut.

"Look," Whit says, pointing to the window at the back of the van. "At least this time they gave us a view. Want to take in some Overworld scenery?"

I shrug listlessly. I can still see Eric in my mind, and all I want to do is stay curled in a ball and just give up.

Then I see Mrs. Highsmith in my mind's eye. And I remember the music. *Positive energy*... beating the blues. So I let Whit help me up.

Now I can see what's going on.

We're speeding down an empty six-lane highway with those New Order billboards lining both sides — giant ones, every tenth of a mile or so. It's kind of hard to stay positive watching all of this pathetic crap — His Resplendent Baldness cavorting with upper-level bureaucrats, unveiling plaques to renamed Freeland cities: ONETOWN, NEW ORDER ACRES, VICTORYVILLE, BRAVE NEW ESTATES. It's no wonder Beaners look so glassy-eyed and out of it 24-7.

I'm ready to sink back to the floor when the monotony is interrupted by a giant message in horrifyingly bright-red New Order lettering.

WE INTERRUPT THIS PROGRAM FOR AN IMPORTANT ANNOUNCEMENT.

CLASS I CRIMINALS ELIZA AND BENJAMIN ALLGOOD ARE IN CUSTODY.

STAY TUNED FOR EXECUTION EVENT DETAILS.

THIS IS ANOTHER GREAT DAY.

And there, in the middle of the video displays, are my parents—in orange prison jumpsuits, gagged and shackled.

My knees buckle, and I sink back to the floor.

Chapter 43

Whit

AS WISTY FALLS to the floor again, sobbing against my pants leg, I keep my face pressed to the glass, waiting for the details of the *execution event*. I don't actually want to know, but I have to know. How much time do we have? To find our parents, to plan our escape?

But we're in between billboards now, and traffic is slowing down. I pound the back of the van in frustration. I'm about to crumple on the floor next to Wisty, but I'm suddenly jolted alive with a rush of—

Celia.

It's her scent, no doubt about it. The perfume she wore the day she originally disappeared. It's like she's right here with me, like she never left.

I've never heard of a portal in a moving New Order vehicle. Is it even possible? I start pounding on the floor, the walls, then the back van doors, shouting her name.

"Whit, *stop it*." Wisty looks at me with red, weary eyes. "Celia's gone. You've lost it. Our parents are scheduled for execution! Why are you—?"

But I'm pounding the window again. I see her hair. Waving across the next billboard some hundred yards away, streaming in front of her face.

Whit, Celia says. Her voice is muffled, as if it's coming through a loudspeaker outside. *You're okay. You're doing the right thing. Don't give up.*

I hurl my body against the door. "Get us out of here, Celia!" I know, at least I *think,* it's nuts. How can she be a projection on a billboard? But she's so real. And I can smell her.

Are you even listening to me, Whitford All-good? I said, you're doing the right thing.

I don't even care that she sounds annoyed. I love it. It reminds me of when she'd start telling me about her chem test in the hall at school, and I'd just give her a kiss right in the middle of her sentence. *"Are you even listening to me, Whitford Allgood?"* she'd say, and I'd feel seriously warm all over.

Am I listening to her now? I am actually. The sound of her voice is like a drug I can't get enough of.

The van is getting closer to the billboard. My face can't be pressed any harder against the glass, my body flattened against the door. We're passing right by her image, and I practically feel the heat of her breath on my cheek.

You need to turn yourself in, she continues. *And you're on your way to The One right now. It's the only way. If you want us to be together again, it's the only way.*

"Together again?" I ask.

"Together again," she repeats as we pull away.

And then she's gone. But I'm still dazed by the lingering image of Celia until we turn in through a very high gate marked BUILDING OF BUILDINGS.

Chapter 44

Wisty

WHIT AND I MAY have electrodes all over our arms, but at least we're upright and sitting in high-backed leather chairs so comfy it's like swimming in butter. And we each have a glass of water next to us. It's all five-star accommodations here at the Building of Buildings, which is basically The One's crib and bat cave–type place, and it's where the very grumpy men in the van brought us.

Maybe I could get used to this?

Whit and I had both been curled in the fetal position in the back of the van when suddenly we were yanked out and escorted into the B of B. So this had started out as one of our most pathetic public parades into captivity yet.

I actually made eye contact with some of the citizens who were watching as we trudged across the luxuriously outfitted marble lobby. Maybe I've been infected with a big-ego savior complex, but I thought I saw a flash of… respect, maybe even admiration, or at least something vaguely hopeful buried deep in some of the glazed Beaner eyes. It helped me get my groove back anyway.

The more I stare at our interrogator right now, the more I think maybe I see it in him, too. Grudging respect? He's hiding it pretty well, though. He's definitely polite but sterile to the point of being scary.

The questions have also been pretty sterile so far—such as name, address, and N.O. ID number. *As if* we have an address or carry N.O. IDs!

Then he throws this real doozy at us.

"Have either of you had any children in recent months?" he asks, deadpan. We both stare at him blankly. "Now that we have you and your parents on death row, we need to ensure there are no other living members of Clan Allgood. Please answer so that the polygraph can register a result."

"No," we both manage to say.

"Excellent," he says, watching the readout from the lie detector.

"I get an A plus for not being an unwed pregnant teenager?" I say. "Wow. Maybe I like the New Order after all."

He completely ignores me. "Now let's get down to some very important business. On a scale of one to five, with five being the most, how would you characterize the efficacy of your parents' instructions to you vis-à-vis harnessing your...abilities?"

"What are you talking about?" I demand. "As *you* said, *let's get down to business.* Tell us when our parents are due to be executed! Are they being held here?"

"Ms. Allgood," he says. *Ms. Allgood? Never in my life...* "I'm afraid I am the only one permitted to ask questions here."

"News flash, mister. I'm not big on following rules!"

Whit nudges me as if he's signaling I should settle down. Since when is he going all Golden Boy again? We're Resistance leaders, aren't we?

The interrogator clears his throat. "We *know*

your parents trained you. And we *know* they imparted to you certain, uh, highly sensitive pieces of information and/or equipment having to do with the scientifically proven energy forces that you both possess by dint of your genetic makeup."

"Are you talking about *magic?*" I ask. Whit frowns. *Mute* Golden Boy.

Mr. Interrogator looks extremely alarmed. "Shhh! Take my word and do *not* use that term in this building—or anywhere! You're living very dangerously."

Perfect invitation for me to get punchy. I'm practically singing at this point: "Magic, magic, magic, *magic, ma*—"

The Repressed One finally explodes. He's up and grabbing us by our collars, my shirt in one hand and, surprisingly, that of my Mute Golden Boy brother in the other.

"You make me *ill!*" he practically spits.

He looks at Whit. "You, with all your potential, and look what you do! Nothing! Sitting here like a mannequin! And your dynacompetent sister, here—why, she possesses a power so amazing, so devastating, so—"

There's a sharp noise as the automatic dead bolt on the room's door clicks open.

"Ah," says our interrogator, suddenly whiter than a pickled egg. "Said too much, did I?" he whispers to himself. "Oh!" he manages to squeal as somebody steps softly into the room behind us and the temperature drops, oh, maybe fifty degrees.

And just like that the interrogator turns into a medium-size rubber tree in a large terra-cotta container. Somebody has just made him into the quintessential potted plant.

And I have a good guess who.

Chapter 45

Wisty

INSTANTLY, IT'S AS IF someone's quadrupled the gravitational force in this place, and the energy's leaking out of me. I can't even sit up straight anymore. He has these electrifying *Technicolor* eyes—you've never seen anything like them. They'd be, like, *model* gorgeous if he wasn't so evil. As it stands, they're like an instant barf inducer. I'm queasy. But Whit's still locked into his weirdly placid state.

The One Who Is The One steps around the table, sliding our former interrogator's pot into a corner of the room with one foot.

"He'll need some watering," he says to nobody in particular, and then smiles silkily. "Or *not*."

The One waves at the far end of the room and transforms what had been a featureless white wall into floor-to-ceiling windows. He can turn a man into a plant. He can fly. He can vaporize children. I guess turning a wall into windows with a panoramic fiftieth-floor view must be a walk in the park.

"Now," he says, eyes briefly pulsing red but then turning a charismatic blue—a shade you might see on some touched-up face in a magazine ad (that is, if they made magazine ads for Pure Evil).

"Come," he invites as if we're old friends. He gestures at the picture windows. "Have a look."

"Um," says Whit, "we're kind of hooked up—"

But all the polygraph wires are now gone, like they'd been particularly unlikely figments of our imaginations.

The One beckons gently. "I think you'll enjoy this," he says. I'm shaking now. The One seems to "enjoy" nothing except torture and death. *What's up his sleeve? And what's up with my brother, for that matter?*

Whit gets out of his chair and walks over to The One like an obedient child.

"S'all right, Wisty, come on." *Does he have some intel I don't?* Last I heard him say more than a few words, he was bouncing off the van walls with rage.

But I don't want to be sitting over here alone. "For lack of anything better to do," I say begrudgingly, "okay. Let's have a look."

"Why the impudence?" The One asks. "You do know I *don't* intend to kill you." He puts his creepy, long arms around our shoulders and leads us to the windows. Strangely, his touch feels totally warm, even a little reassuring.

"Will you look at that?" he asks almost wistfully. "Do you see how the sky and the mountains there seem to be joined? Almost seem to be *one?*"

We gaze out across the city, the foggy street and building lights twinkling through the gloom. The clouds on the horizon are a sinister purple that does kind of merge with the snowless mountains beyond the valley.

"Do you have any idea how much work it took to make this perfect evening?"

I start shaking again. It's as if he's a cat playing with mice. He just said he wasn't going to kill us, but is he about to anyway? In any case he's definitely going to put some serious hurt on us.

"I bet you're wondering what I mean by that," he goes on. "A terrific high-pressure zone had been screaming down across the northern plains and would have brought torrential downpours tonight. Possibly even hailstorms."

We look at him blankly.

"So I *stopped* it."

Now I get it, and what he's done is pretty mind-blowing actually.

He raises his arms to point at a cloud on the horizon, and with the most casual of gestures, *he steers it in over the city.* Now he's making a spinning gesture with his other hand, and the cloud rotates. And now he's guiding in another massive cloud, and another, and another.... Soon there's an enormous swirling, lightning-streaked vortex circling over the entire city.

As it churns and intensifies, the winds start rattling the windows. My ears pop as the pressure in the room drains. Does he plan to have us sucked up into the black core of the vortex? Is that tonight's plan? The rain is crashing down in iron-colored curtains. The building is groaning on its foundation. Is he going to vacuum the entire city off the face of the Earth?

But then he snaps his fingers, and the storm moves in reverse. The spiral turns backward and de-intensifies, and then the clouds retreat to their original stations in the sky.

"Now, you try, Wisteria," he says.

Chapter 46

Wisty

"WHAT?" I'M CAUGHT off guard—completely flabbergasted. Then it gets even weirder. Suddenly it's as if I'm at my piano lessons again, and he's Mr. John Masterson, my sweet-as-pie teacher, encouraging me to believe in myself. Say *what?*

"You have more than enough power to do it. Just tell the energy what it should do, and let it out. You saw what I did. Give your power that same image, and let it go. I have every confidence in you and your wonderful Gift."

He's out of his mind. Turning people into animals is, I admit, pretty cool, but it's, like, *finite.* Graspable. I can't wrap my mind around the sky, the wind, clouds, hurricanes—that's big-time.

"I can't do that," I whisper.

"*Now*, Wisteria," he says, a tone of threat creeping into his recently soothing voice.

I close my eyes and try to remember exactly how the clouds raced in over the city, how they joined together and began to swirl like an upside-down, ink-filled toilet flushing in the sky, the lights of the city twinkling below and almost disappearing as the rain whipped down. I let the tune of Mrs. Highsmith's song work as a soundtrack as I imagine it all playing before me.... *Can I actually do this? More important, do I want to? How can I live, and be the same person, with so much power?*

And then I feel my heart flip inside me. My whole *being* flips.

"*Idiot!*" he screams.

I open my eyes. The clouds are exactly where they were. The only thing that's changed is that the city has gone entirely dark; even the lights in the room are out. We're bathed in evening shadow.

"You put out the lights, Wisty. *All* the lights," whispers Whit.

Chapter 47

Wisty

THE ONE IS PAST polite whispering. "You turned off the city's electricity!" he screams. "Reactivate it *immediately!*"

I try, but I don't know how I did it in the first place, much less how to reverse it. *Hum Mrs. Highsmith's song backward?* I can't. I'm panicked.

"You chaotic *child!*" he says. "You really don't have a shred of control, do you? Now The One Who Manages The Power Grid and his incompetent minions will be spending hours attempting to repair what you so blithely have done!"

I'm madly trying to think of a poem about

light dawning. *There* must *be one! Why is my mind like a slushie when I'm around The One?*

He pauses as some deeply unpleasant thought settles into his mind.

"Do you have any idea how much power it takes to do what you've just done? Or the applications to which such an ability might be put? Do you?"

He grabs my head in his long-fingered hands. It's no longer a warm touch. His skin is so cold it stings. He's hurting me now. A lot.

"Time for a pop quiz, my dear Wistful," he says ominously. "Do you remember anything, anything at all, from your Biology 101 class? How about physics? Chemistry?" His hands are pressing harder into my temples.

"I...must've...skipped...those," I manage to eke out through my clenched teeth. This is pain like I've never experienced before.

"Ah. I should have expected as much from a truant. What a shame that you know so *little*," he spits out, "about your Gifts. About how the functioning of the human mind, and thus the body, is controlled by electrical impulses. Electricity, in a sense."

The One's coldness extends invisible tentacles *inside* me. Ice is growing down my spine. "And I...should care...because...?"

"You. *Foolish. Child!*" he screams, shaking my head now, practically crushing my skull. "You have no respect for what you've been given!"

I try to flame up but realize I can't. He's entirely *draining* the magic from me. All the warmth is slipping from my body. Like I'm dying. He's actually killing me right now, isn't he?

My legs buckle, and a whimper squeaks out of me. Whit snaps out of his trance and swings around in alarm to help, but The One lets me drop and fends him off with an elbow. The One's mere touch sends Whit sprawling back on the floor and slamming up against the far wall as if he is a rag doll.

"All that power inside you," The One Who Is The One says, his eyes once again flashing pure evil, "to control the mind.

Everyone's minds. *The entire world* at your fingertips."

Suddenly the cold stops, and he backs away with a rueful smile.

"I frankly don't know whether to be *im*pressed or *de*pressed."

Chapter 48

Whit

I'VE BEEN HIT PRETTY HARD during a few N.O. attacks, but right now I feel like I've been ploughed into by a speeding truck. Wisty's on the floor looking spent, but then she hauls herself up. She's okay, thank God, but apparently still too dumbfounded by The One's completely absurd claims to say anything.

This is my chance. My one chance to find out what Celia was talking about. I just wish I'd had time to figure out how to broach the subject first with His Oneness.

"Um, excuse me?" I use the wall to help steady my body as I peel myself off the floor. "I have a question. Excuse me?"

Wisty and The One both stare at me as if I've just risen from the grave.

"I need to ask you about Celia Millet." Hearing her name aloud, here, in the Building of Buildings, feels so . . . *ancient.* From another time and place. So out of reach, despite how close she'd seemed just hours ago.

"Celia Millet?" He raises his eyebrows. He knows her name. But he pretends he doesn't. "I can't possibly keep track of all the pernicious children we've had to process through our retraining systems. I'm afraid I can't help you. Was she a"—he smiles condescendingly—"*special* friend?"

"You know exactly who she is. She told me to come here. To turn ourselves in—for our parents' sake." It's probably insane, I know, but I take a deep breath and say it. "We need to talk about a deal."

"Whit?" Wisty is agape, agog, astonished, every word you can think of for "in total disbelief." "Are you *high?*"

The One just laughs. And laughs, and laughs.

"Well," he says, finally recovering, "it looks

like we have one boy suffering from post-traumatic stress disorder and one girl with..."
He chuckles again. "Developmental disabilities, of a sort. Thank heavens we rescued you before your conditions got any worse. It looks like both of you need a little...recuperation. And *education*."

I can't hear him. I shake my head. "I need to talk to you about Ce—"

He speaks right over me. "And it just so happens I have a new facility designed for just that purpose. I think you'll find it much more suitable than your last accommodations with us. Call it a spa, if you will. I'm sure your sister will enjoy it, at least."

He casts an amused eye at Wisty. "Perhaps they can even help you with your unfortunate— *hair* situation, Wisteria." Another nasty snicker. Wisty growls as if she's trying to turn into a werewolf. Whatever it is, it doesn't work.

"Listen." I finally collect enough energy to take a stride toward him. "I'll go to your stupid school or whatever if we can strike a deal."

"Ah, but you're going regardless, Whitford!

First, though, I'll need to ask that you hand over any personal property—like that journal you have under your shirt."

He raises his snaky fingers at me, and the journal flies out from where it was tucked under my belt. And as the book zooms right into The One's grip, I find myself flying backward and slamming into the wall. Again. And it really hurts—*again*.

"There is no power in the pen and page anymore, my friend. Remember that. There is only power in *energy*. Now let's see what you have in here," he says, licking a finger dramatically and riffling through the pages. "*Po*-ems?" He starts to chortle. "And, oh my goodness, they're *bad* poems—listen to this one!"

Out—out are the lights—out all!
  And, over each quivering form,
The curtain, a funeral pall,
  Comes down with the rush of a storm,
While the angels, all pallid and wan,
  Uprising, unveiling, affirm
That the play is the tragedy, "Man,"
  And its hero, the Conqueror Worm.

He laughs as if his sides are going to bust open. Unnaturally glittery tears spill down his cheeks. "That," he says, struggling to form words through his fit of amusement, "is the most pathetic, juvenile thing I've ever read!"

Wisty gives me a look that says she knows it's a poem by one of the most famous poets ever, the darkly inspired Edmund Talon Coe.

"Well, clearly you couldn't write your way out of a paper bag, so go ahead and keep it, you pathetic poetaster."

He flings the journal back at me. I make a perfect catch even though I'm still getting my wind back.

"And you," he says to Wisty. "Hand over the stick, my girl. I'd like to finish what your dear friend Eric, may he rest in peace, began."

Wisty goes gray at the mention of the drummer's name, and grayer when she tries to process The One's implication. She's already gripping the drumstick tucked in her back pocket, but her fingers fly open and the stick zips through the air and into his waiting hands. He considers it for a moment and then fakes a little one-handed riff.

"You look pretty natural," she says as her face clouds with anger. "What's your stage name again? The One Who Can't Get A Recording Contract?"

"You!" he screams. *"Are . . . not . . . funny!"* He takes the stick and breaks it in two, flinging the remains at her feet.

"Bully!" she yells, dropping to her knees.

"Tsk-tsk," he clucks. "I assure you that *names* will never hurt me, Wisteria. Now," he says, swiping the broken drumstick out of her hands before turning to leave, "somebody come and get these two ready for the school bus!"

Chapter 49

Wisty

ALL RIGHT, so I'll admit it. There was a very small part of me—the dream-big girl who'll cling to any hope no matter how many times she's been crushed by the cruel heel of life— that hoped we *were* headed to some sort of spa.

I mean, I wasn't expecting a mani-pedi while drinking a seltzer with lime, but I let myself imagine something low-key, like being a quarantined tuberculosis patient at a convalescent hospital, sitting on a porch wrapped in a blanket, staring out at the countryside.

But that was the very, very old days, and this was a very, very new world. As noted by the name of this facility.

"Welcome to the Brave New World Center," intones a disembodied female voice as we step into the brightly lit, ultraclean entryway of our new home. Stun guns are planted firmly in the smalls of our backs.

"Please prepare to watch the Brave New World Center Onboarding Video," continues the voice. She sounds like a computer-designed voice-over—a little *too* perfectly modulated. With any luck, maybe she'll shut up and we'll start watching calming videos of waterfalls and rain forests, or maybe she'll conduct mind-body relaxation exercises.

This whole place actually looks more sanitary than a hospital—white glossy floors, white glossy walls, white glossy ceilings. "What gives?" I ask Whit. "I thought there was a New Order law that said they always had to put kids in filthy hellholes."

"Clean hellholes apparently will work in a pinch," says Whit.

"Who knew? I'm waiting for my white terry-cloth robe and fuzzy slippers."

"Shut *up!*" barks one of the guards behind us.

The lights go down as orchestral, sound-track-style music fills the room, and the wall in front of us lights up with images. The disembodied female voice comes back. "Congratulations on your admittance to the Brave New World Center," she says. "The most advanced facility of its kind in all of the Overworld, dedicated to the nurturing of young dynacompetents. Built in the Year 0001 A.O., the BNW Center features the latest in new technology and employs the best pedagogical program ever devised for unlocking scalable kinetic potentials and directing them into a life of fully compliant productivity."

My eyes are glazing over already. Maybe she *is* inducing hypnosis. . . .

The screen plays a video tour of the immaculate hallways, classrooms, lecture halls, cafeterias, and dormitory rooms that presumably await us beyond this reception chamber. Everything reeks of sterility.

"The curriculum features twenty-four-hour audio- and video-based instruction." The screen flashes images of hundreds of different speakers and monitors — in the corners of ceilings, along walls, in desks, in headboards. "In this way, lessons will continue uninterrupted — even during sleep. Ninety-nine point three percent of students find they are able to absorb enough information and behavioral training to evolve to the second level in *less than two weeks*."

"Big whoop," I hear Whit mutter. "Dogs in obedience school do better than that."

I start to snigger until he suddenly yells, "Ouch!" and jerks his hand up in the air. From out of nowhere a small robotic thingy has scooted up and smacked his knuckles with a long yellow bar that looks suspiciously like a ruler. Maybe it's a stun gun.

"And," continues the woman, "as a means of ensuring that the BNW Center remains a one hundred percent optimized learning environment, you will find in place a system of corrective negative feedback stimuli for any disruptive or wasteful behaviors. No student has ever been released from the Center without complete mastery of the core curriculum!"

"I'm still waiting for my aromatherapy treatment," I whisper to Whit.

"Your *what*-atherapy?" he whispers back.

Thwack! Thwack! Zoomba, the little robot thingy, is back with its stick.

Now Whit and I are both sucking our knuckles. So much for my spa fantasy.

"This concludes the Onboarding Video. Again, welcome and congratulations on your admittance to the Brave New World Center. Won't you have a chocolate?"

The little robot in front of us has lost the ruler and is now holding a tray with two chocolates on it.

Okay, so my spa dream is back in play!

I guess if they wanted to poison us, they could have done it already, and I'm not sure I care either way at this point.

I pick one up and — *OMG* — it's the best-tasting thing I've ever had inside my mouth. I'm seriously about to collapse in a heap of unending lip smacks and mmmms when the door in front of us clicks and in walks... *Byron Swain.*

Chapter 50

Wisty

"HEY, GUYS," says Byron, weaseling up to me and Whit with an air of, I don't know... there's something slightly off about him. Dejection, maybe? "They told me to come... welcome you."

"How'd *you* get here?" I say, with a tone wavering between disgust and bafflement.

"Does it matter?" asks Whit, glaring at Byron and nudging me. "We're all here now." And I think I know why: *to defeat the New Order from the inside.*

I notice that Byron's practically swimming in his all-white jumpsuit, as if it's a hand-me-down costume carelessly pulled off a pile rather than carefully selected.

Suddenly I realize Byron might be on a mission to free us. *Better be nice to the guy.* "Cool outfit, B.," I comment, then decide that I'm not a good liar. "You look ridiculous."

"It's the school uniform," he tells us. "You'll have yours as soon as you get decontaminated."

"Decontaminated?"

"Cleanliness is next to Oneliness," says Byron. The guy has no sense of sarcasm about him. Makes him impossible to figure out.

"So the brainwashing's going pretty good with you, huh?" I ask.

"It's not so bad," replies Byron kind of listlessly. "There's chocolate, you know."

"Calling that stuff 'chocolate,'" I say, swallowing a mouthful of saliva in afterthought, "is like calling caviar 'fish eggs.'"

"When did *you* ever eat caviar?" asks Whit.

"There are a lot of things you don't know about me, Brother."

"I know you sometimes pretend like you've done things you've only read about in books."

"It's not *totally* pretending. When you read a book that's good enough, you sort of *have* done the things you read about."

"Don't talk about books," warns Byron. "You don't even want to know what they do to you here for that. If ERSA hears you—"

"Who's Ursa?"

"The Educational Remediation Services Administrator—the entity that runs, or really *is*, this place. That's the voice you were hearing over the intercom. And nobody's ever seen her in person, so some of us think she's just a computer. An extremely powerful one."

"I knew The One was into technology, but actually having a computer run a school—that would be a whole new kind of insane."

I glance over at Whit, who's staring at one of the little spots on the wall. There's one every few feet, and up in the ceiling, too. And each is covered with glass.

"Camera lenses, or ERSA's eyes, if you prefer," says Byron. "You'll get used to it. Although, word to the wise, it's always best not to forget you're being watched. Almost always."

"Almost?"

Byron shoots me a look. "Actually, *always*, always. I wouldn't want to face the wrath of ERSA myself."

I burst into a squeal of laughter. "Oh, it's my worst nightmare—a computer gone ballistic! Can't wait till Mrs. ERSA whips my butt when I tell her she can go *reboot* herself." I'm guffawing at my own incredibly stupid joke.

"Don't laugh. You'd be surprised what she can do. Like, she can change the chemical composition of the air in this room if you're not compliant—even make it toxic. And she doesn't care who else is in the room with you."

"Seriously, Wisty," says Whit, hushing me. "Try to keep the attitude in check. We need to *not* make waves if we want to figure out what's going on in this place."

"Um, Whit, this isn't us on some sort of mission. This is us being *prisoners*."

"Fine. You go ahead and get busy figuring out what kind of special punishments you can earn. Meantime, I'm going to keep my head down and my eyes open."

"Awesome," I say, my tongue finding some chocolate residue still wedged between my molars. "And I'll keep my eyes open for more of *that stuff*."

Maybe it's time for me to turn over a new

leaf. Maybe it won't be that hard to keep my mouth shut to earn some brownnose points. Come to think of it, I'm not above acting like my last name's "Swain," if it helps me nab more chocolate.

I twist my head around at the sudden sound of the rear wall parting, revealing two arrows—one pointing left and marked with a ♀, and the other pointing right, with a ♂.

And ERSA's voice fills the air. "Informant Swain, return to your quarters. Whitford and Wisteria Allgood, you will now proceed to the gender-appropriate decontamination showers for cleansing."

Informant?

Informant?

My body is already charged and whirling with vengeance, my chipped fingernails ready to start clawing at that traitor's eyes with reckless abandon.

But he's already gone.

I'm really going to kill that kid.

Chapter 51

Wisty

ALL RIGHT, we're definitely on the inside now. Maybe Whit is right, maybe this is the only way to defeat The One. Maybe we're closing in on something important. Meanwhile, though, we look like freshly boiled lobsters.

"Ow, ow, ow, ow, ow!" I'm jumping up and down as Whit and I are reunited in the (surprise) all-white common space, waiting for our next instructions.

"Stings, huh?" Whit agrees. "I have to admit, though, you really needed a bath. You were kind of starting to stink."

I punch him in the arm. Apparently even near-death experiences can't take the obnoxiousness totally out of the brother. "Speak for yourself. And they seriously didn't need to take off the top two layers of my skin to solve the problem."

Byron, on the other hand...I remember a murder-mystery board game we used to play as kids, and I start a wicked fantasy: *Wisteria Allgood, in the shower, with the industrial-strength power nozzle...*

My plotting is interrupted by a military march–like set of notes signaling the end of class, then the sound of a bunch of kids emerging into the hallway. Several come into the room and plop themselves in front of a TV.

"Hey, guys," says the boy who sits down next to us. "I'm Crossley." He's short and wiry, with a boyishly earnest and appealing face.

"I'm Whit, and this is Wisty," says my brother somewhat guardedly.

"Yeah, everybody in this place knows about you two. Especially Wisty." He leans in. "Saw you rockin' out on the Net."

Whit and I are stunned. "Huh?" says Whit. "How'd you—?"

Crossley's eyes flash toward one of ERSA's

eyes. "Anyway, they gave us all chocolates when they announced you were coming."

"Do they give chocolates often?" I blurt out.

"Every once in a while ERSA gives them to the whole school, but usually it's just when you earn a trip to The Room Where You Eat The Chocolate."

"So how do you earn that?"

"By being a good student, generally."

"Like solving trigonometry problems?"

"Sort of," says Crossley. "You'll see. The chocolate is awesome. It's just that some of us aren't quite prepared for its...awesomeness." He turns his attention to the TV screen and pastes a smile on his face like a baby who's just been fed, pooped, and changed.

I suddenly realize that I have no idea if the kids at this school are brainwashed New Order spawn — Mini-Ones in training — or if they're innocent kids trapped in a white N.O. box just doing what they need to do to survive.

As Crossley cheers along with the group at another exciting ribbon-cutting ceremony being broadcast on Channel One, I notice him discreetly holding up a small scrap of paper, shielding it in the palm of his hand so that the cameras can't see it.

I KNOW A PLACE WHERE ERSA CAN'T HEAR US.

Another mindfreak. For the past few months, my Enemy Meter had two readings: *For Us* and *Against Us,* with His Traitorness Swain spinning the thing into overdrive. I'd wished all kids were For Us. I'd assumed it. But now?

"Maybe I can help you guys win the next competition. Come on, let's go study!" I look at him as if he's crazy, but then I notice he's winking at me. *Ew.*

We follow Crossley out of the common room, down a couple of hallways and stairways, and ultimately to a spot just between the A Barracks and the B Barracks. He quickly points at the walls, which, for a few yards, have no cameras or microphone knobs.

"The emergency-containment doors open here, so they didn't install any cameras or mikes," he whispers. "So, if you want, I can tell you what I know about your parents."

In the blink of an eye, Whit has him by the collar. "What do you know about our parents? Where are they? How do you know?"

"Whoa, boy!" Crossley gasps. "You don't want to hurt me. There's a lot I can do for you...if you cooperate."

"Cooperate how?"

"Make a fair trade. I get some of your M; you find out from me where in this facility your parents are being held."

Whit gives Crossley a perfect body slam— enough to scare him but not enough to really hurt him. "I repeat, *what do you know about our parents?*"

"Whit, *chill*," I whisper, trying the, um, feminine touch instead. "Look, Crossley, you seem like a nice guy. We don't want to hurt you. But you know what? We *can*. You're lying about our parents. We'd never be put in the same facility with them. So first, stop lying, and second—what do you mean by our 'M'?"

"Your magic. Your mojo. Whatever. I need

some. I'm flunking out and need help." He gives us a pathetic look, and Whit eases his grip. *"Please."*

Someone's asking *me* for help with his "schoolwork"? I'm just about to burst into hysterics when an alarm goes off.

ERSA's voice echoes through the hall: "Code gray. Code gray. Code gray."

Crossley squirms out of Whit's distracted grasp. "Air-quality alert. Bet it's an escape attempt," he says, and starts tearing down the corridor. "In five secs this hall will be swarming with guards!"

The emergency-containment doors fly open and slam Whit and I against the wall behind them. Three school monitors the size of nightclub bouncers are dragging escapee Byron Swain. He's limp — *dead?* No, he's coughing now. Hard.

He sees me, of course, and croaks, "Told you. Stay away from the wrath of ERSA."

Chapter 52

Wisty

MY FIRST CHOCO-OPP IS a contest taking place in the Dynasium—basically a gym for dynacompetents, which is what they call kids they think might have *energy capabilities* rather than admitting that we actually have *magic.*

There are weights to levitate, bottles of various liquids to transmogrify (yeah, I don't know what that means either), metal bars to bend, braziers of oil to set alight. And there are bunnies and rats in cages for I don't know what yet—maybe we'll just have to change the color of their fur?

Crossley, who's now pretending yesterday's weird episode never even happened, tells me the kids call these competitions "*spell*ing bees," although that's strictly on the down-low. So is the slang term "M," for magic.

ERSA, like most New Order officials, has absolutely no sense of humor. So we're not in here casting spells, you see, we're here demonstrating "dynacompetent potentials" and transmitting "biokinetic energies."

ERSA's smooth-as-apple-butter voice fills the room. "Students, join your partners at the workstation identified on the assignment board and await further instruction. You will have sixty seconds to complete your assigned challenge."

I look up at the board and moan aloud. Whit got some cute girl named Cherry Lu whom he's been playing eye hockey with ever since we got here. And me?

Perfect.

I have Byron "Nonmagical Weasel Who Shouldn't Be in This Place to Begin with" Swain. "Informant" Swain. "Soon to Be a Half-light" Swain.

I take a deep breath so I'm better able to resist the urge to strangle him. *Focus, Wisty.*

You must win the contest, I remind myself. *Do it for the chocolate.*

Byron and I head over to our station, a wooden bench with a series of lightbulbs and some big old metal drum attached to it. As we walk, I actually put my arm around his waist—but it's only because I've got a pencil in my hand that I'm knifing into his side as hard as I can.

He doesn't resist.

"I hate you forever," I say through gritted teeth. *"Forever,* you hear? You're a criminal. An informant on Freeland. You're probably the reason Whit and I ended up here."

Byron says nothing. He just looks...sad.

"On the count of three," says ERSA, "you will turn over the instruction card at your station. The first team to successfully complete the task it describes will win a trip to the BNW Reward Center...for chocolates. Get ready!"

I shove Byron out of the way and give him a threatening look so he knows not to interfere. "You're probably the reason Eric betrayed me," I continue.

"One..."

"And the reason that Margo died," I accuse him. "You're a *murderer*."

"Two..."

"So what do you have to say for yourself, you hideous, low-down *louse?*" I place my hands on either side of the laminated instruction card.

Byron looks me in the eye.

"Three!" ERSA announces.

"I promise you, Wisty," Byron whispers, "everything I'm doing is to protect you, not to hurt you. I swear to you over my dead body. And I will be dead, soon enough. I would even die for you."

I turn over the card and... *No way.*

Good afternoon, ma'am. Flame Girl reporting for duty!

Chapter 53

Wisty

IT WAS TOO EASY.

The apparatus on the table was a steam turbine hooked up to a generator, and, get this, all I had to do was use magic to heat the thing up to light the bulbs on the table. I lit those bulbs so bright the other kids started yelling at me to turn them down because it was hurting their eyes.

Sore losers.

Not that I blame them — I'd be honked off, too, if I wasn't going to get any chocolate.

I'm so pumped I don't even care that Byron's coming, too. And, I have to admit, his very traitorous presence ticks me off so much it's easy to light up every single bulb that I walk by on my way out of the Dynasium.

I hardly notice that the "Reward Center" looks like some enormous, dingy corporate call center with carpet-board cubicles all over the place. Sitting at many of them are blissed-out, brown-mouthed children, with enormous platters of chocolate in front of each of them. The kids are covered with wires and weird electro-majiggies that sometimes seem to pulse with a strange blue light.

But, OMG, I can *smell* the chocolate! Mouth watering. Knees weak. Can't talk.

"Prisoner Allgood and Informant Swain, please proceed to cubicles 124G and 124H," says ERSA.

"Follow me," says Byron. "I'll show you how to hook up the monitors."

"Monitors?"

"You need to wear the monitors when you eat the chocolate."

"Not surprised, I guess, that you're so skilled in surveillance tech," I snort. But just between you and me, right now I'd wear an I ♥ BYRON

T-shirt if it meant I could get some more of that chocolate.

Byron helps me put these little suction-cup things on my forehead and arms. They're like those electrodes they use on patients in the hospital, only they're bigger, and the wires are a whole lot thicker.

And then, *Oh yeah,* here comes an automated cart with two huge platters of chocolate—I'm talking bigger than my head! One has Byron's name on it, and the other—

I've wolfed down at least a quarter pound before I even realize I've done it. The stuff tastes *that* good.

And I'd suck down more except my stomach is starting to protest. I guess there's a reason people don't eat candy for breakfast, lunch, and dinner.

I take a breath and look around.

Some of the kids have clearly been here awhile and have eaten their entire trays. Most of them are now slumped over. *Napping, I guess?*

Except maybe that little kid over there—he definitely looks a little green.

And that girl lying on the floor. While I watch, two goons in medical scrubs come in and drag her away.

Byron looks up from his own personal choco-fest and notices my glance.

"Yeah, she probably hasn't learned her limit yet. They'll take her to the vomitorium."

"The *vomitorium?*" I ask, not really thinking it through.

"That's what the students call the place where they pump your stomach."

"Ah," I say, vaguely finding that disturbing, but I feel another choco-craving coming on and quickly turn my attention back to my glorious platter. I swear, if they'd had this stuff back in my high school, I would have weighed 250 pounds.

But right then I start to get really tired, and the suction cups on me — it's as if they've gotten very cold. They're almost *burning*, the cold stings so much. The wires are glowing an unearthly blue color. And my stomach's totally knotted.

And I don't know that I've ever been so tired

in my whole life. It's as if these wires are sucking the life out of me....

Byron is giving me a worried look. *What's he saying?* Maybe if I just put my head down on the desk for, like, a few seconds, just close my eyes...

Chapter 54

Whit

POOR WISTY COULD BARELY SIT UP and, for two days afterward, had to stay in her bunk, subsisting on water and the soup crackers that I stole from the cafeteria.

But the craziest and scariest part of it was, even in the height of her sickness, she was *still* craving more chocolate.

My sister was officially an addict.

"I actually fantasized before we got here that it would be like a celebrity-rehab center where I could just do nothing but recover all day," Wisty confesses to me at one point. "Now that I'm doing it...well, it sucks."

It's not easy for a champion athlete and a whip-smart troublemaker who loves the spotlight, but we resolve from here on out to be the most average, unremarkable students in the building.

We'll do everything asked of us, but no more than that. Nothing that will make us stand out. Anything to keep us from getting any special attention.

It's nearly impossible to stay under the radar with Crossley and Byron on the premises, since we'd love nothing more than to interrogate the heck out of them. But we quickly figure out that the best strategy is to nod politely and do our work with as much mediocrity as possible.

Our assignments center around the "brilliant efficiency" of the New Order's world vision. Essays in which we prove that The One Who Is The One is the most powerful visionary in all of human history. Math problems in which we demonstrate that never before have more people been more productive than under the New Order. Science readings in which we learn that magic, art, music, and most of the rest of humanity's former extracurricular activities were harmful to humankind.

One day our plan to blend in goes up in

smoke, though, when Crossley does something really stupid. He's still peeved at Wisty for not giving him some of her M.

We're sitting in the cafeteria, eating the usual nutritious but antidelicious porridge, when he throws a piece of chocolate out on the table right in front of her. I figure it must be stolen, since he doesn't get to the Rewards Center much.

"Want some choc-o-late, Wisty?" he says real slowly, smacking his lips.

My sister looks down at the candy and literally starts to tremble at the temptation. She drops her spoon and grabs the edge of the metal table with both hands.

"Yeah," Crossley goes on, despite the "I'm going to grind you into burger meat" look I'm giving him. "I won a contest. Guess I didn't need your help after all. But maybe I could use your help eating my rewards," he says, pushing the chocolate closer to her. "Or not." He pops it into his mouth.

Wisty's shaking. In fact she's shaking so hard the whole table's moving around. And now, oh no, not *again*—

She bursts into flames.

Chapter 55

"FINALLY!" SAYS THE ONE Who Is The One triumphantly. "This is what I needed to see.

"Clearly," he continues, walking away from one of the dozens of video monitors, stroking his chin, "it's just as I hypothesized. It appears she manifests especially in moments of great duress. Which clearly indicates she has little or no mastery of her Gift."

The man at his side types this up in his mobile data pad and nods.

"Once they've doused the flames, put her in the Isolation Ward. We need to study her abilities in a controlled environment. And, needless to say, show no mercy. Not to either of them. I need results, results, *results!*"

"Yes, Your Excellency," says the assistant.

"The Allgoods believe they're here to get closer to me, and they're absolutely right," The One reflects. "In time, once I know them better than they know themselves, I will get very, *very* close to them."

Chapter 56

Wisty

"WELL, 'GRIM' HAS A new dictionary entry," I comment aloud to myself as I explore my latest venue. The Isolation Ward they put me in is actually the vast, windowless, unbearably dank basement of the BNW Center. "This place makes the General Bowen State Psychiatric Hospital"—one of the dungeon cribs that we busted out of—"look like a flower shop, a tea parlor, and a cribbage hall."

Great. Five minutes in solitary, and I'm already talking a blue streak to myself.

No worries, though. My giant bunker is about to be filled with six bighearted scientists running inane tests on me. You know how your doctor bangs your knee, shines a flash-light in your ear, and presses your tongue down with a stick and never finds anything wrong? It starts out kind of like that. The medicos seem particularly interested in my fuzzy head, examining it with a magnifying glass.

"A shame that the original was destroyed," a giantess I decide to call Helga says to another "researcher," who looks like a beautician from a backwater town—who nearly flunked out of cosmetology school. I call her Gigi.

"The informant has provided a small speci-men, but the rest is said to be lost, or possibly under heavy guard," says Gigi.

Am I actually hearing that my hair has become like the Holy freaking *Grail?*

Then someone starts plucking out some samples of my hair—or, rather, reddish stubble—with a tweezerlike tool.

"Ouch!" I yell, and try to slap the hand away, but my wrists are grabbed by a doughy-faced lab assistant I call Hans.

Gigi, who I think is the lead scientist, steps back and looks intrigued, almost pleased, by my reaction.

"Why don't you just wax my whole scalp while you're at it?" I spit out sarcastically, and then instantly regret it.

Because that's when the torture really begins.

Chapter 57

Wisty

IT BEGINS with the waxing. Helga takes the hot substance and sticky fabric strips and starts ripping the eighth-of-an-inch-long precious regrowth right from my skull. Okay, it's my scalp, but it feels like my skull.

Note to self: Never make torture suggestions to captors. They have plenty of their own creative ideas.

As in, testing my response to sudden, random eardrum-breaking air-raid sirens. Or to lights that strobe really slowly so my eyes nearly adjust to the darkness and then—*flash*—I'm blinded by an eye-exploding random pulse of pure white light. It's truly the stuff that migraine headaches are made of.

"If this were an interrogation," I tell them, "I'd have given you your answers long ago. So what are the questions? I repeat, *what do you want from me?*"

"Give us your Gift," Gigi demands. "That would be sufficient."

"No way!" I wouldn't do that even if I knew how.

While Gigi executes the experimentation, Hans and Helga hold me in place as needed. Their three white-suited compatriots are now sitting in a row of chairs in front of me with their notebooks, watching as if I'm the season finale of their favorite TV show. The only thing missing is the popcorn.

Next they're delivering hot steam into my face and nostrils like a facial from hell. Suffocation by dragon breath. Give me waterboarding any day.

Then they demonstrate an acute pinching technique that takes six hands — Helga's, Hans's, and Gigi's — and if that sounds like child's play, think again. It's like being attacked by fire ants with road rage.

"Give us your Gift!"

"WhmmaMMMMMphhhhhh!"

I forgot to mention — they seem to need to try everything twice: once with duct tape on my mouth/eyes/hands, and once without. This time, it is *with* duct tape.

Then there is the force-feeding of unmentionables (I can't even write it without serious gagging). Let's just say I would rather be biting off live bat heads.

What ends up being the worst part, you ask?

If you have an aversion to dismemberment, don't read any further. (Okay, that pretty much includes everyone.) While my limbs remain intact, someone else's apparently haven't.

They bring Drummer Boy's hands. On a platter.

I know from his insignia ring. They force me to hold those hands, and, by God, they are real.

I used to think that the New Order had banned all art, but I now realize I was wrong: *The fine art of human torture is alive and well here.*

Chapter 58

Wisty

THEY FINALLY GIVE UP on me. At least for now. I curl up in a tight little ball, trying to recoup my energy for when they come back. The endless hours of drip-drip-drip quiet are interrupted only by the occasional scuffle of a rat, the noise of the grate opening in the food chute, and the *thunk, thunk, thunk* of a loaf of stale bread and a semifrozen block of lima beans descending to me.

Yes, lima beans. With freezer burn.

I pick up the crumbling block, and I'm startled by what I think sounds like a sizzle. Must be my imagination. It reminds me of when I was six, when Whit and I plotted to steal Mom's lima beans out of the freezer and flush them down the toilet without her knowing. We succeeded with part A, but not part B. And guess who got in trouble? Me. Always me. And *still* it's me, alone in my punishment.

Whit, I need you here now! I hurl the chunk of beans at the door with a power I didn't even know I had, and it shatters with a satisfying crunch.

"Uh-oh." I hear a voice from behind the door. "You okay in there, Wist?"

Whit?

"Whit?" I shout, running toward the door as I hear a key in the lock.

In comes my brother, escorted by a chunky school monitor. Much to my amusement, the guy actually slips on a couple of lima beans as he enters the room but tragically doesn't fall flat on his face.

"Jeez, Wisty, what happened to your head?" is Whit's greeting.

I'm hugging him in an instant, and then I see who's being escorted in behind him. Sporting a black eye. *How predictable is this?*

I glare at the weasel. "I thought this was supposed to be *solitary.*"

He glares back. "Don't blame me, Wisty. It wasn't my decision. Ask your brother."

I let Whit go as the grunting monitors shove their wards into the basement with me. Without a word they leave, the door clicking and locking behind them.

"What *happened* to you two?" I ask, not entirely hiding my delight at their imprisonment, or really at the fact that I have some company, which, as you probably know, misery *so* loves.

Whit shrugs. "Byron and I got in a good old-fashioned fistfight. You know. Guy stuff."

"Well, good for you, boys. And good for me. I have company now!" I spread my hands out grandly. "Welcome to my little shop of horrors. They do free head-waxing here, by the way. I'm sure they'd do your chest for you, Whit. And your monobrow, Byron."

"That's vile," Byron remarks, picking up a lima bean from the dirty floor and examining it.

And it's going to get a lot more vile down in this dungeon.

Chapter 59

Wisty

I'M CLUTCHING A LIMB, or I guess I should say a dismembered arm. *Drummer Boy No More's.* Then suddenly it's pulsating and starts moving as if it's a living thing, first caressing my face, then, like the traitorous soul it belonged to, clawing viciously at my eye....

I wake up screaming and with my head pounding. Even worse, Byron is leaning very close to my face. I can smell his dippy cologne. "Are you okay, Wisty? You're as white as a sheet and you're sweating like a soaker hose."

They've clearly given Byron some sort of script that's been diabolically designed to keep me on an emotional knife-edge between suicide and murder.

The dayless, lightless monotony down here also creates the ideal conditions for psychosis. We've already taken bets on who'll succumb first. Byron's been — I kid you not — counting beans (lima beans, that is), just like his deadbeat New Order dad. Whit's been writing in his journal and searching for the Shadowland (and Celia, of course), and I've been self-inflicting pain in order to steel myself for the next visit from the torture brigade.

"Make him go away, Whit," I grunt through my headache.

"Really, Wisty," insists Byron. "I just want to help—"

"I don't need help. I'm perfectly capable of being miserable on my own. Buzz off and do something useful for once in your life," I mutter.

"Something useful?" he says. "Oh. I didn't think you thought that I could."

"Seriously, I'd be *so* incredibly psyched to be proven wrong right now."

"Well, then. How about…I pick the lock on the door?"

Whit and I both look at him, trying to figure out if he's joking. Then I remember: Byron has a subzero sense of humor.

In our exploration of this dank place, we've come across only three doors. And, of course, they've all been locked tight. We've checked, in the event that there's some good-hearted, *normal* person hiding in the body of a grunting, surly school monitor. *(Not.)*

"I did it on one of the other doors—not the door we used to get in here," Byron explains. "Then I put it back so we wouldn't get in trouble."

"A door is a door is a door," I say, still aghast. "How'd you *do* it?"

"It wasn't that hard. I used to be a Sector Leader's Star of Honor, and as trainees we learn all kinds of skills that are helpful in a prison. So I found a piece of wire and I looped it into the tumbler and felt around, and then, you know, before too long, I'd got it."

"When exactly did you do this?" I ask.

"When you guys were snoring so loud that I couldn't sleep."

"Let me get this straight," says Whit. "You can pick the lock to a door that might be our escape route out of here, and you didn't tell us?"

"Well, there's something behind the door," explains Byron.

"So? Like what? A monster?" Whit quips and makes a scary face.

"More like, umm..." Byron's voice trails off.

"What?" I scream at him.

"Your parents."

Chapter 60

Whit

I KNOW YOU'RE ASKING yourself the same question I am. I'm sure Wisty is, too. Could there possibly be *any* reason *not* to tell us that our parents are in the room next door? *If they really are?*

"I...I think they'll hurt you, Wisty," Byron stutters. "They're not safe anymore. Something's happened to them."

That's all just total bull. Has to be. Byron is clearly the first of us to go psycho.

I put my arm around my sister, and she's shaking with dread and fear. "Not safe? They're our *parents!*" Her voice is becoming shrill. "They're not capable of hurting us. I swear, Byron, if it turns out you're not lying and you can get us to them, I will *kiss* you over and over. And forgive you for every single awful thing you've ever done. Which is a lot."

That makes it a no-brainer for the weasel. With a sigh, he starts toward the door, and we follow. Could Crossley really have been telling the truth?

"Swain, you're not getting off that easy," I call after him. "If you're lying, I swear you'll regret if for the rest of your days. And if you're not lying, then explain why you think they're dangerous!"

"I can't explain it," he says, and seems about as disturbed as we are. "Some things you just can't explain. But it's true."

"Our parents are good people. They haven't changed," I tell him as we arrive at the door. "Just...do your thing, Byron."

Byron's trembling—in real or acted fear, I don't know or care—but he nods and sticks his piece of wire into the keyhole and starts feeling around.

After a small eternity, we hear a click.

Chapter 61

Whit

I GRAB THE HANDLE away from Byron and press down on the thumb latch. We're greeted with another click, and then I slowly push open the creaky door.

Unlike the rest of this forsaken pit, the corridor ahead isn't even dimly lit. It's pitch-black.

"Can you see anything?" Wisty asks from behind me.

"Let your eyes adjust," Byron suggests. He's hanging back a little, clearly not thrilled that he suggested this little plan but complicit now. "You'll see. I think."

After a pause, my heart stops for a beat.

There's definitely something moving in the darkness ahead of us.

"Mom? Dad?" I call out tentatively.

Wisty takes my words to mean I think I've seen them, and she bolts out from behind me.

"Mom! Dad!" she cries.

I feel her flying by me in the dark. "Stay *back!*" I shout, and with a lucky reach, I catch her by the sleeve of her jumpsuit. Just in the nick of time, too.

Because right then I hear the loudest, most terrifying growl.

Wisty's breathless. "S'okay, Whit," she whispers. "I'm good with dogs."

"It's not a dog." Byron's voice drifts in. "Trust me on that one."

It's the *next* voice I hear that sends my heart racing. Or skydiving.

"Whit? Wisty? Did I hear your voices?"

It's our mother!

"Yes, Mom!" Wisty calls into the dark. "We're here! Are you and Dad okay?" Wisty is struggling to get free of me, but I won't let her go yet. This can't be safe. Something's very wrong.

Then our mother says, "Don't come near us! Get away!"

I can feel it now. Something really bad's going to happen.

Our mother and father don't want us here.

Chapter 62

Wisty

A FLICKERING COLD BLUISH LIGHT from *I don't know where* suddenly illuminates the end of the hallway. It's like a scene in a horror movie shot in monochrome.

My parents — gaunt, sunken-cheeked, listless — appear to be shackled to a far wall. My mother's formerly thick and curly hair looks flat and matted with sweat. Her eyes are bulging as she stares, alarmed, into the darkness. *She's not seeing us, is she? I don't think so.*

And my father's eyes are...closed. His body is so thin, and he's limp. *Is he—?*

I can't even begin to imagine this. It's so wrong and impossible to comprehend.

"Dad!" I scream again. And that's when I

see a hulking animal emerge from the darkness. My mother yells out a second time, "Go back! I beg of you! Get *away* from us!"

The creature starts pacing in front of our mother and father. Whit's grip on me tightens. The creature's flesh is falling off, its mouth drips blood, patches of its skull bone are sticking out all over the place through patchy, mangy fur.

Whose blood is that on its muzzle? Don't let it be my mother's and father's—

Suddenly the light in the shapeless space is brighter. I see that the wires hooked to my parents are glowing blue, eerily like the ones in the Reward Center where they sucked me dry.

"We have to take out that *thing,* Whit! Now! I'll do it if you won't."

Byron's voice urgently whispers from behind, "No, Wisty! It's a spirit-sucker—a Lost One. If it gets you, you're done! Even you can't defeat it."

"I don't *care!*" I scream, struggling harder against Whit's grip. "I'll burn you, Whit. I swear I will."

"Wisty, just wait a sec." Whit's eyes have

been locked on the scene in shock, but now he lets me go. "Ow!" he yells. "You did it!"

I'm glowing. I'm getting hotter and hotter. I'm a firebrand. Maybe, just maybe, my M is rising? "I can do this. Mom and Dad, I'm coming to get you...don't worry!"

"No! Turn back!" Mom moans. "Get away! I'm warning you, Wisty! You, too, Whit!"

I start tearing down the corridor, and Whit is just a half step behind me. I knew he'd fight! The creature turns to face us and starts bounding toward me. I see bloody, clumped, rotting fur swinging under its jawbone. Then I blast through a virtual wall of its foul, stinking breath.

As I take a flying leap toward the creature, all I'm thinking of is a tigress tackling a rabid jackal in the wilderness, concentrating on the sensation of claws pushing through my fingers, sharp enough to rip this horrid beast apart.

Please, please, let my magic work —

And then I'm engulfed in fur, bone, and teeth.

Chapter 63

Wisty

THE SECOND THAT WHIT lands on top of me, we body slam the floor and the room goes dark. Everything is gone. The creature, Mom and Dad, the eerie blue light—all of it. And then...all is explained.

"Well, well, well." We hear a voice behind us. And it's not Byron's. "Once again, you have ruined everything, Whitford Allgood."

Whit and I are still recovering from the impact and seeing stars, but that dimly backlit caned figure, combined with that frighteningly familiar voice, equals bad news, the worst news possible.

It's The One, of course, standing there in his dark business suit, long arms folded, right in front of me and Whit. Byron the Traitor Weasel is nowhere to be seen.

"Wondering what I'm doing here? Taking time away from my frighteningly full schedule?" he goes on. "Well, I'm afraid I received a call from the school headmaster. Seems you've not been the model students we'd hoped you'd be. Just when you, Wisty, had a chance of making a breakthrough, your overzealous brother crushed it. I mean that quite literally. I was *this* close to securing Wisteria's Gift."

Whit's still holding me, but I manage to struggle up, squinting, dazed, the horrid vision of our parents lingering with me.

"Breakthrough?" I choke out. "Are you telling me that whole horror show was just another *test?*"

"I'm not *telling* you anything, Wisty. At this point, I've lost my patience with you."

"Wha—?" So maybe my parents *aren't* actually near-starved war refugees guarded by a Lost Thing? This is good! My heartbeat is settling.

"What do you want from me?" I demand.

"I aced your test in the Dynasium and then got so sick that I almost vomited up my toenails. That's about as good as it gets. I'm no A student."

"How wrong you are, my Wistful. I should have known you would have ignored what I taught you about the true potential of your power. We had higher hopes for you, but you've proven yourself to be just another teenager who disrespects the guidance of her elders. So *terribly* sad." He sighs. "I daresay you deserve some punishment for wasting so much of society's time and resources. But where do I start? So many ways to punish, and so little time." He chuckles. "Perhaps we'll begin by vaporizing your friend."

My stomach drops. I immediately think of Janine. Or maybe he means Emmet...

"Mr. Swain!" The One announces.

"What?" Whit blurts out.

"I will now disintegrate your good friend Byron."

I'm so twisted with all of the horror, anxiety, and relief of the past few minutes that I can't help bursting out with a laugh. It's a nervous titter, but a laugh nonetheless. Inappropriate, yes. And maybe even a little insane.

His Coldness drops his arms in utter surprise and looks at me with undisguised hatred. *"What is so funny?"* he bellows. "Your humor misses me completely."

Whit's laughing now, too. "Go ahead," he says. "Weasels are immune to vaporization anyhow." As if demonstrating that *he* is the first to succumb to isolation psychosis, Whit starts pantomiming a jumping weasel, dodging vaporization rays. So I keep laughing. I mean, it looks really ridiculous.

The One Who Is The One stares at us, dumbstruck. "Fine," he says quietly, and turns to me. "In that case, it will be *you!*"

I stop laughing. So does Whit.

"I'll admit I'm rather pleased by the results of my experiments with your parents so far. I've been getting stronger and stronger…and *they,* well…you've seen the fantastic results." He gestures toward the scene of our latest mindfreak. "Even if it was a holographic projection. My latest dynacompetent mastery, by the way." He breaks out in a self-congratulatory smile, which I return with a glare. "At this rate, I may not even *need* you, Allgood children. So I present you, Wisteria, with a deadline: twelve hours. Exactly twelve hours to manifest The Gift in a manner in which I may...partake of it. If you don't, it will be *you and your brother* that I execute."

And then, with a wave and an incantation, he chills the whole basement with a heavy snowfall—*from the ceiling*. The temperature plummets at least fifty degrees.

"That should help you concentrate," he says. "I feel that the cold works wonders on most students." And he swirls out of the room.

Chapter 64

Wisty

AND THE SNOW JUST keeps falling.

My new definition of evil: anyone who makes me hate something that I love. Such as: I think I might hate chocolate now. That's criminal. It's the BNW Center's fault. I think I hate Celia for driving Whit half mad. Definitely the N.O.'s fault. Now The One has made me hate snow. Which I used to adore.

I remember how, every snowfall, Whit and I would be outside finding a way to go sledding, no matter how old we were. The only thing that changed was how daring we'd get, even going down hills that had a "frozen" (we hoped) pond at the bottom. In recent years he'd even drag Celia along, and I must admit,

I loved watching the two of them together. They were so happy being with each other.

Those were the days. Days where nothing scared us.

Now snow will only symbolize these harrowing last moments leading up to my death.

I've found a few wooden boards, which I've stacked up so I can sit on them, to delay the frostbite on my butt cheeks from huddling on the floor. At this point we are already in about three inches deep. My forever-heroic brother keeps exploring the basement, looking for a way out—or for a new portal. Meanwhile I've been trying to recite every poem, song lyric, or nursery rhyme I've ever committed to memory. I know these schools have some sort of "magic-dampening" properties, but it seems as if we've almost always found a way to use our powers, at least a little, if we tried hard enough.

It's the cold. I know it. I freaking *hate* the cold. And now it's literally going to be the death of me.

"Okay, Whit, get out your journal!" I call to him. "I'm going to dictate my Last Will and Testament."

"I'm listening." Whit's muffled voice drifts over from a corner of the basement, where he's rapping on the wall like a detective, only one who doesn't really know what he's doing.

"Write it down! I'm serious."

"Wisty, I hate to remind you, but...we *ain't got nuthin'* to be willing to folks," Whit drawls, coming toward me with some discovery in hand. "Or folks to be willing 'em to."

"Don't be dark. That's my job. And may I remind you that somewhere in the world are two halves of my drumstick. I would will them to you, but you're gonna die, too, so I need a realistic backup plan."

Whit arrives with a piece of canvas just large enough to wrap a corpse in. "Found this," he says, throwing it around me. "It's not much, but—"

"If it'll delay hypothermia for even five minutes, I'll take it. Thanks," I say, holding out a corner so he can slip in next to me. "So, you ready to write?"

Whit looks at me with a surprisingly even gaze, no trace of Celia madness in his eyes, thank God. I need his sanity now. "Sure thing, Wisty."

He pulls out his journal and a pen, and I clear my throat dramatically. "I, Wisteria Rose Allgood, hereby declare my Last Will and Testament."

Chapter 65

Wisty

I PAUSE AND LOOK at the falling snow, beautiful in kind of a fake way, and remember that time when nothing scared me. And now I'm not scared anymore of what's going to happen. I'm at peace.

"First of all, let it be known to the world — and to the Curves and Half-lights and Lost Ones and even the New Order zombies — that I'm a witch and proud of it.

"All of my powers, whatever they are, I hereby bequeath to my dearly beloved brother, Whitford P. Allgood, for as long as he gets to live. No one else. Period. I'd rather have a Lost One dismember me limb by limb than to have my powers extracted for the New Order."

"Aw, shucks, Sis," Whit says with mock modesty.

"I leave my drumstick, should it ever be found, to my mother. If no Allgoods survive me"—I shiver a little—"I leave it to Mrs. Highsmith. Rock on, very cool lady. Next, I leave my wig to Janine. You don't have a clue how beautiful you are, girl. I used to kind of gag on your crush on Whit—"

"Do I really need to write that?" Whit breaks in.

"Every word."

"Then slow down."

"Okay. So, Janine. After the part about gagging, write: Now I dream of you two getting married and having lots of little rebel babies together." Whit rolls his eyes. "Further, I leave my electric guitar to—"

"Wait a minute. You don't have an elec—"

"Shut up. Let me dream for a minute, okay?"

Whit nods.

"I leave my electric guitar to Sasha. I forgive you for lying to me 'cause now I really do understand why you did it. There's nothing more important than fighting these arrogant and obnoxious N.O. fiends. I'm sorry if I let you down in the end."

I'm feeling the melted snow seeping through my saturated sneakers now. *Black toes, here I come.* I curl them tightly back, as far away from the wet chill as possible.

"And Emmet. Man, I miss you already. You make everything better just by smiling. I wish I could leave you everything you deserve. A new world. Or, rather, the old world back. Instead...I leave you...my hair."

Whit starts to protest again, since I have no hair, but I give him another "shut up and keep writing" look.

"I hope you didn't trash it after the hack job. Apparently they're treating it like the Holy Grail now. It's the only part of me that'll be left after they vaporize me. Maybe if the world ever gets normal again, you can auction it off on uBay."

"To some rabid Wisty fan who'll pay a million beans for it," Whit suggests.

"As if—," I start.

"I know just the person who would," Whit

says, and then the person Whit's thinking of shows his sorry, sad face in our sad, sorry space.

For all of his faults, Byron has absolutely flawless timing.

Chapter 66

Whit

"I REQUESTED THE HONOR of bringing your last meal to you, Wisty," Byron says quietly to my sister, seeming genuinely humble.

He glances at me apologetically for once before mumbling, "You, too, Whit."

He crunches through the snow toward us, rolling a wheeled cart that makes a very irritating squeaking noise.

"More chocolates for Wisty?" I say sarcastically. "They nearly killed her the last time. Maybe the third time's a charm?"

"Could you skip the meal and bring me an extra-extra-large ski parka and snow boots instead?" Wisty sniffs and wipes her running nose on her white jumper.

Instead of answering, Byron lifts the hotel-style metal cover from the tray, presenting it awkwardly, as if we should be more interested in eating the lid than what's underneath it.

Wisty seems to be reading Byron's mind and squints at the underside of the lid, but my attention is drawn to the pathetic scraps on the plates. "Boiled potatoes and vitamin bars?" I mutter. "That's not a last meal. That's all they *ever* serve in this place."

Wisty and Byron's eyes are locked, and she's staring at him with a deeply disgusted look on her face. And I don't think it's about potatoes.

"Well, then," he responds. "Maybe we can...spruce this meal up a little together." Byron is shooting me one of these "Don't you get it?" looks.

Wisty gently nudges me and nods at the lid Byron is still holding up. Attached to the underside is a note:

> WISTY, I LOVE YOU. I WON'T LET YOU DIE. I THINK I CAN HELP YOU. I *PROMISE.* NEED TO GET AWAY FROM ERSA FIRST. HOPE I CAN DO IT.

"Here, I tell you what...," Byron says, rolling the cart toward a faraway dark corner of our vast prison. "Let me bring this over here for your...convenience."

I hope ERSA is stupider than we thought, since there is absolutely *nothing* convenient about eating in one of the darkest corners of the basement.

I take Wisty's hand and drag her off the boards, knowing she'll need some coaxing to be in the dark with Byron after his declaration of love. I figure this is our last chance. We're desperate enough to take help even from Byron the Weasel with the Lovesick Heart.

Once we're in our "dining room"—a tiny nook under the stairs—Wisty doesn't hesitate to grab a boiled potato and cram it into her mouth. *"Garçon?"* She pretends to be flagging a waiter. "Can you bring some bacon, cheese, and sour cream over here to go with my potato? *Tout de suite!"*

"Wisty," he whispers urgently, but so quietly I'm convinced not even a bug planted right on his person could pick it up. Dang, he's good. No wonder the guy's practically a professional double agent. "I didn't mean to alarm you with my note, but you had to know the truth, so you'd believe me when I tell you I can help. Probably."

I don't need to have night-vision goggles to sense the daggers flying from Wisty's eyes. "Pardon me if I'm asking the obvious, B., but whose side are you on anyway? It's, like, the last burning question I have before I die."

"Okay, listen. I've figured out something incredible," he goes on. "I believe that the times you've used your powers on me... *have changed me.*"

"No kidding, Swain," I hiss. "Get to the point, or get the H out of here."

"Your magic... I think... it can sort of... rub off. I think I have some small degree of your power now that can rejoin with yours... and become... like, greater than the sum."

Wisty pauses, trying to absorb this latest bizarre info dump. I expect her to drop a bomb, but she's actually listening. "Like... maybe I've... given you a kind of... electrical charge?" I can't believe she's starting to regurgitate Onespeak.

"Maybe. I don't quite know. Here, let me show you. Quick. I need both of you to take a hand—we need to be touching."

"If this is just a ploy to hold my hand, B., you're dead," Wisty says.

"Concentrate on the food," Byron orders. "Dream of what you want. Wisty, say something."

"Um…" She whispers something under her breath, and I have a pretty good idea of what it might be.

I still can't *see* anything, but in a matter of seconds, I *smell* something unmistakable. Cheeseburgers, onion rings, and—I think—black-and-white milk shakes. It's strong enough to make my knees feel weak.

"How'd you *do* that?" I ask Byron.

"Remember the prophecies?" he says. "Have you ever wondered how an army of kids might possibly prevail against the New Order's army of soldiers—with their guns, their tanks, planes, and ships? What I've started to understand at this place is that, unlike New Order soldiers, we're overflowing with ideas and creativity and potential."

Once again Wisty surprises me with how she seems to get where Byron is going. As much as she hates the guy, they do seem to have some weird connection. I felt it when they were onstage making music together. I'd never tell her that, though.

"The One Who Is The One is scared to death of us and our potential. Our *energy.* That's what all the schools and prisons for kids are about." Byron's voice picks up volume with excitement, and he has to quiet himself down. "He wants to figure out how to steal it, which is what this place is for. Failing that, he wants to remove the threat."

"How can you steal somebody's potential?" I wonder aloud, not expecting an answer.

"That's what he's trying to figure out. He wants to unite with Wisty—"

"Ew," my sister interjects. "Ew, ew, ew, ew!"

"Silence!" screams ERSA suddenly, and she's sounding quite a bit more human—and stressed-out—than I've ever heard her. "If there is any more nonessential speech, you will spend the remainder of your time gagged and shackled!"

Chapter 67

Wisty

BYRON IMMEDIATELY RELEASES his sweaty hand from mine. Or maybe it's my hand that's sweaty. After all, death is really close now. *Really* close.

"ERSA," Byron calls out, proceeding from our dark dining corner to a slightly less dim area of the basement, "the condemned have requested use of a proper bathroom. One last time… before the execution. I've refused the request, but they've been insistent. What should I do?"

I've heard about last meals, but last potty breaks?

"They may not leave the basement," says ERSA, but then I swear I hear her sigh. *Can a machine sigh?* "There is a toilet behind door B12. I will release it for five minutes."

"Yes, ERSA. I'll accompany the prisoners to make certain they're..."

Byron trails off as a door in the wall clicks open. "Compliant."

Next, Byron sweeps us into a room about the size of an old-fashioned telephone booth. "Quick. We need to hold hands," he says.

"But I haven't gone yet," I protest. I actually do need to use the toilet. As you might imagine, I'd been avoiding crouching in a corner. With no toilet paper.

"You don't have time to go. We need to use your magic ASAP."

"And why would it be working now?" Whit asks. "We've been trying to use magic since we got here."

"You saw what happened with the food. I haven't figured it all out yet, but there's something about the power that was transferred through Wisty to me, I think." *Great. I turn the guy into a weasel, and he gets the ego of a lion.* "Maybe it's like evolution. Each generation develops new characteristics to cope with new forces in nature—"

"Generation? Cripes, Byron, it's not like we had a *baby* together—"

"Just be quiet and hold me, Wisty. This is serious."

Talk about evolution...is this really Byron Swain coming to the rescue—again? He's changed. He clutches my hand, and his feels warm and confident.

Byron turns to my brother. "Whit, do you believe me?"

"I hate to say it, but what choice do I have? Sure, Byron. Do what you can."

"You two have nothing to lose. And neither do I—I'm dead regardless. Quickly now, look for a spell. Something about...water."

Whit opens his journal and flips through a few pages. He finds an entry he likes.

Although you hide in the ebb and flow
Of the pale tide when the moon has set

And here's the weirdest thing: the air is kind of hurting my lungs a little; it's too dry or something—

The people of coming days will know
About the casting out of my net

Whit's face — I don't know how to describe
it — it's gotten pointy, and his lips seem over-
size and —

And how you have leaped times out of mind
Over the little silver cords

Byron grabs the journal out of Whit's hands,
and I gasp. My brother's skin has gone silvery,
and something bizarre is going on with his
neck. It's as if he has . . . scales?
Byron finishes the spell:

And think that you were hard and unkind,
And blame you with many bitter words.

We're turning into fish! What good will
that do, ending up as fish on the bathroom
floor?
Have I trusted Byron one too many times?
And why is he so huge all of a sudden?

Then there's this unusual popping sound, and... the two of us are resting in Byron's outstretched hands, looking up at his giant face.

We've apparently turned ourselves into guppies. And now we're 100 percent relying on Byron to go find us a fish tank?

"Wisty," Byron's voice seems to boom inside my head. "I meant what I wrote. I love you. I know you think it's the worst thing you've ever heard. But I can't help it. You're everything I always wished I could be. Funny, relaxed, strong. Smart, rebellious, and you don't care what others think—unless it's your family. You know what's important. You're perfect."

I'd love to say *Thanks, B.,* but I'm seriously drying out here. My skin, my mouth, my *gills*...they're all stinging like mad.

"You and Whit are on your own now," he continues. "I know I won't make it out of here alive. Not when The One finds out what I've done."

Suddenly we're moving away from his face and toward a white porcelain bowl.

"Good-bye, Allgoods," Byron says. "What I do now, I do for love!"

Chapter 68

Whit

PLOP!

Plop!

Terrific. We've just been dumped headfirst into a toilet—and a gross one, too.

And before Wisty and I even have a sec to take a lap around our "wading pool," up through the refracting surface of the water I see Byron reaching for the toilet handle.

God, no! That traitor isn't going to—

But he is. And when you think about it, considering the downward spiral we've been on lately, getting flushed down the toilet really may just be the ultimate poetic justice. I still can't figure out if the creep is saving our lives or just getting a kick out of flushing down the pipes his former nemesis and the girl who'd so often rejected him.

But when the full force hits, none of it matters anyway. After the shock of the initial crash of water, which comes close to knocking me senseless against the sides of the pipes, it's one dark and scary shot straight out of the school building. The water power is so strong I can't even twist my head far enough to see if Wisty's behind me. It's killing me not to know if she made it.

I'd been a champion swimmer in school, so the sensation of being a fish isn't as odd for me as I might have thought. But this is like trying to do laps in an ocean during a *hurricane,* so no, I've never trained for it. And I'm worried about how Wisty's handling it... until I remember that she's done time as a rodent in a gutter.

Wisty, hang in there, I'm thinking. *Just remember to breathe.*

The pipes are getting wider and wider, which doesn't offer much relief since there's these waterfall noises that keep getting louder — and the too-gross-for-words stuff coming down the pipe with us is getting thicker and thicker. Just the thought of it makes me nearly suffocate.

Just remember to breathe, Whit, I say to myself. Which is actually pretty good advice, because when I do, I realize that my sense of smell isn't on a human scale.

So I breathe even more deeply, and I catch sight of Wisty. At least, I assume it's her and not some other guppy busting out of "prison" via the sewer.

We make eye contact, and I think, *Follow me,* hoping that the message somehow comes through in my face. I'm glad we've spent so much of our lives understanding each other without saying a thing.

We're going faster and faster—a real raging river—until suddenly we find ourselves in still water: a storm sewer. From there we make our way downstream and into a maze of lazy subterranean canals under the city.

Before long Wisty and I see something we haven't seen in a long time—light! Real, honest-to-God daylight! We stare at it, mesmerized as it grows and grows. We start to see blues and greens and yellows and—

Why is the light growing so quickly when we're not even swimming hard? And what's that almost deafening, roaring sound?

"*Swim back!*" I try to scream. But I can't. I'm a fish.

And it's too late anyway.

Chapter 69

Whit

YOU KNOW THOSE NIGHTMARES where you're falling and you're entirely helpless and you wake up with a start? This rush is kind of like that, but not.

It's *not*, because it's *not ending*.

There's no control. There's nobody to help. I can't even hope to see Wisty in this powerful, downward-spiraling torrent. All I know is that I'm lodged inside a *roar* with nothing to hold on to but my useless panic.

Faster, louder, faster, louder, and then — *bang*.

And then — *uhh*.

My guppy brain feels as if it's come unattached from the inside of my tiny little fish skull. I think I just did sixty to zero in point two seconds.

And then all is calm.

Calm . . . and *sunlit?*

I'm outside?

In one piece? I think so.

Why am I not surprised that the environmentally unfriendly New Order has a sewer that goes directly into a river without any filters or processing facilities that would grind two innocent little guppies into crop fertilizer?

For the first—and hopefully last—time, I'm thankful for their complete lack of morals and civility.

I'm in a lazy bend in the river, and, despite the toilet water that the New Order has clearly been pumping into it, it's still totally beautiful.

Lily pads and their brilliant white flowers float around us lazily. Spiral snails slide along the rocks without a care in the world, and a brilliantly striped turtle slips off a log and glides by like a stubby-legged flying saucer.

Suddenly I realize I'm seeing this with eyes that are above water. I'm floating . . .

Like a dead fish, or a living human being?

I jolt up onto my feet and realize I'm alive and human again, standing in about three feet of water. The spell must have worn off. I whisper a prayer of thanks to Mom and Dad, who I feel are out there, watching over us somehow. Then I give quick thanks that the spell didn't remove my white Brave New World Center jumpsuit, which is now sopping wet.

I swirl around, looking for Wisty. *Thank God—there she is!* She's just now hauling herself up the wooded bank of the river. She's dazed, but her eyes light up when she sees me.

"Whit!" she calls. "Wasn't that...wasn't that just the most amazing ride ever?"

Chapter 70

Whit

IT MIGHT NOT SURPRISE you to find out that I wasn't just an athlete in the old days, I was also a fourth-degree Falcon Scout. So I know that generally when you're lost in the woods, the first job is to find shelter.

But on a night as perfect as this one, we're not stressing about it.

We've already walked several miles — west, back toward Freeland — and though it's starting to get a little cool, we're just going to sleep under the stars.

The sun has dipped below the horizon, and things are starting to get pretty dark. From here on out, we're strictly going to be feeling our way around.

"Bring a flashlight?" I ask my sister jokingly. "We could use it to find two sticks. And then we could rub them together, and—" Suddenly the tree trunks ahead of me are flickering with dancing orange light.

I spin around to face Wisty. And there on the ground, with my sister sitting cross-legged in front of it, is the most perfect campfire I've ever seen, complete with encircling stones and a nearby stack of wood.

"Fire looks a little hot," I say, referencing the six-foot-high flames nearly licking the overhanging branches of the trees.

"No problemo," says Wisty and, as if she were turning a dial on a stove, drops the flames down to a more manageable foot or two.

"And without your drumstick," I observe. "I'm impressed."

"Yeah, well, I've always done better out of school," she says. Her pale face is flushed, glowing. She looks like she's just risen from the dead. "I know it sounds dumb, but it feels so good. To just be able to use my power. Without being crushed. It's like I didn't even realize how heavy the weight was until it was gone."

"I know what you mean. I feel it, too." And it's true. Without even focusing too terribly hard, I'm able to produce three hot dogs on the ends of three bamboo skewers. It's almost as if there's been a backup of energy and potential from all that time I hadn't been using any of it.

"Sweet," says Wisty as she takes her dog. "Maybe you *did* learn something at the BNW Center."

"I don't give them credit for anything beyond learning to love lima beans," I joke. "Which, actually, is a handy skill when times are lean and mean. Remember when Mom and Dad were, like, the emperors of discount vacations? I swear we spent more time in the woods than we did indoors."

Wisty nods, and we start roasting our dogs. "Remember that time it was raining so badly and Dad slipped and fell off the path into the swamp and all the food was in his pack and it got ruined?" She laughs.

"Yeah. It was a long hike back to civilization for dinner," I say, but I'm remembering something else now about that day. "Weird..."

"What?"

"I never mentioned this 'cause it didn't mean anything to me at the time. I overheard Dad saying to Mom something like 'We could just solve this the easy way, Liz.' And then Mom said, 'We promised each other never to take the easy way. Especially with the kids. They need to learn the hard way.'"

Wisty takes it in. "You think they meant magic? Or whatever it is that we're doing—'realizing our potential'?"

"I think they didn't want us to just rely on magic to get what we wanted. I guess that's why they didn't teach us about it at all. They wanted us to—"

"Learn to do stuff the hard way? So we'd understand what the rest of the world was going through?"

I nod. "Could be."

"Well, Mom and Dad, wherever you are..." Wisty looks up at the sky. "We're learning the hard way. The really hard way. Hope you're happy. Somehow, I really hope you're happy."

Chapter 71

"I'LL ASK IT AGAIN in case somebody's actually listening this time: do I have to do *everything* around here myself?" demands The One Who Is The One.

The One Who Tallies the Internal Revenues, Byron Swain's father, stands behind him and shakes his head in disgust.

The One's overseers of pedagogical technology, facilities, and discipline are standing over the smashed circuit boards that had formerly contained the ERSA computer program — the system that had been in charge of the Brave New World Center. All three are fairly shaking under the wrathful eyes of The One.

"Your Eminence, it would appear they

escaped through the toilet fixture because Byron Swain—"

"For the last time, and I assure you this *is* the last time I will ever remind you, citizens are *not* to be addressed with Old Order names! These can lead to insidious individualistic tendencies. His name is now The One Who Infiltrates The Resistance Leadership! And *his* punishment will be nothing short of torture, I assure you."

The One smiles at Byron Swain's father, then studies him for a reaction. The man offers not a flinch of discomfort.

"The fact that there are not filters on the toilets, the fact that the dampening shields were not consistently employed, and the fact that this *moronic* computer program of yours decided to grant a *toilet* request to the two most powerful dynacompetents in our custody are just the beginning of where the true failure lies!"

"We're already in the process of correcting those problems."

"Not necessary. Those of us who are competent enough to wear the insignia of the New

Order will deal with this. Those of you not competent shall have the insignia removed. Or, rather"—he chuckles—"the insignia will have *you* removed."

With that, he throws out his hands and vaporizes the three BNW Center administrators—everything, that is, but the "N.O." insignia on their uniforms.

"Somebody pick those up," he says, pressing the intercom button on his desk. *"And send in the Informant."*

Byron Swain is escorted into the room at once. Though his hair lacks its hallmark camera-ready coif and his eyes are puffed with weariness, he holds his head high.

"Your Eminence," Byron begins, looking The One directly in the eye.

The One raises his stick threateningly. "Who *dares* to speak to me before I speak?"

"I do, sir," Byron continues with his steady gaze. "I know I have failed you, sir. I have been a traitor to this Great Order. I fully accept my punishment. I am ready."

The One pauses, then studies Byron. "So very brave indeed! I wouldn't normally expect that from any son of"—he gestures to his minister of internal revenues—"that one."

"Nor would I, sir," Byron says without missing a beat, inspiring chuckles from The One. There will be no more merciless beatings from his father after his execution, so Byron feels empowered to speak the truth for once in his life.

The One is rapt with bemusement. "I like the spirit, boy, I do, I do. I'm so saddened that my dreams for you have been…delayed."

"Delayed? Sir?" Having expected nothing less than death, Byron cannot process his meaning.

"I'm well aware of your…inclinations toward our escaped redheaded witch. Since she rejects you, you wish nothing but to die. To die as the hero that saved her life. So tragic! The stuff of stage drama. Thank goodness we've outlawed all of that whimsical drivel and nonsense."

Byron begins to get nervous. "I wish nothing but to be executed in shame for my betrayal to you, sir."

"You lie!" The One thunders, quite literally,

as his anger shakes the entire building. "Your punishment will either kill you, quite excruciatingly, I might add, or else it will transform you into the kind of man we need for positions of high leadership in this Order."

"Sir?" Byron says again, his throat drying as he feels his well of courage—the one that has taken days to fill—starting to run low.

"You are now officially in charge of the Kill Team to once and for all rectify this situation."

Byron swallows. "The *Kill* Team, Your Eminence?"

"In our efforts to apprehend and control The One Who Has The Gift, we have spent altogether too much time and too many reliable resources—"

"Exactly three point seven million B.N.s," interjects The One Who Tallies The Internal Revenues.

"Such waste!" screams The One. "Clearly my single-minded pursuit of her has been too much of a drain. And so I have decided, since we cannot wrest The Gift from her, we will remove the threat she poses. Put simply, we will kill her. Or, rather, *you* will kill her."

"Sir?" Byron says yet again.

"You started out so well, boy. You impressed me, if but for a moment. Alas, like so many commoners, you've fallen prey to nothing but adolescent physical attraction. Waste, waste, waste! I do so hope that you'll return to your senses.

"Regardless, *you will kill the girl.* Your team will kill the girl. Or else you will bring her back alive, and I will kill her, slowly and painfully, in front of your pathetic puppy-dog eyes."

BOOK THREE

THE
END
OF
THE
ALLGOODS

Chapter 72

Wisty

WHIT AND I HAVE BEEN TRUDGING through a steady drizzle for many miles now, and it seems as if every single tree trunk along the highway has been stapled with posters of us. They're recent pictures—my brother and I in our flashy white Brave New World Center couture:

WANTED for **TREASON, TREACHERY, TRICKERY, WIZARDRY, WITCHCRAFT,** and **POLLUTING** the **ENVIRONMENT** with **THEIR PERNICIOUS INFLUENCE**

"Lord, what a girl has to do to finally get popular," I say with resignation. "It's *so* unfair. At least that mug shot of me is better than my stupid yearbook photo!"

"Even with the bald head? Um, I'm not so sure, Wist..."

"I've decided it's totally fierce," I tell him. "Resistance chic. I think it'll catch on."

Whit snorts. I don't expect him to get it anyway, given his fondness for curvy chicks with flowing locks. With my prison-pale skin—two shades lighter than its normal "freckled and fair"—and my raw scalp and dirty baggy jumpsuit, I'm so totally the opposite of his type.

But Emmet might like it. I bet he would. I miss him—and everyone else in Freeland—*so* much right now.

"Are we there yet?" I quip as we make our way through a portion of the woods parallel to the highway in the outskirts of a small city. I can hear raucous cheering in the distance.

"We're still a few miles off. The border of Freeland is constantly receding," Whit explains.

"I wonder if that's a New Order rally we're hearing or a Resistance rally. Hard to tell in these parts."

"Should we check it out?"

"Let's," he says. "Carefully."

We turn away from the highway and head up a side street that leads into town. After a few blocks, we spot the fringes of the mob, swarming in a park situated in front of a large stone building. We can't make out their chanting yet.

"It's all adults. Clearly not Resistance," observes Whit. "We can't get any closer without being noticed. We're the poster kids of the week around here."

"Well, then," I muse, "maybe we shouldn't be kids anymore."

Whit whistles as he figures out what I mean. "You think you can do it?"

"Maybe together we can," I say, and take his hand. "I've got no plans to enter my geezer years alone."

I remember a tidbit from a poem Dad used to read to us, and I make Whit recite it with me:

When I was young! ah woeful When!
Ah for the Change twixt now and then!

And then...it's the strangest morphing experience I've had by far. Usually it's swift and smooth, as if I'm as soft and moldable as a chunk of cookie dough being squeezed through some higher power's fingers. This time, it's slow and...painful. Creaky. As if my spine is being crunched down, and the rest of me aches in response, right down to the soles of my feet.

Whit groans, equally unexcited about his new body. "Don't tell me this is how years of playing contact sports is going to wreck me in old age." He moans. "My back is killing me. And both my knees. Ouch, ouch, *ouch*."

I try taking a deep breath, and it's just not the same. "My lungs feel...weird...smaller. Cramped up or something." Suddenly all of Mom's griping about me not standing up straight enough somehow seems to make sense.

The odd sensation of something tickling my neck makes me jump, and I smack what I think must be a spider but what turns out to be—hair! I take a coarse strand in my newly veiny hand and check it out. It's whiter than an ash heap!

"Bye-bye, Resistance chic!" I sing woefully.

"Well, I guess you don't need to worry about growing your hair back," Whit comments.

"And I guess you *do*," I retort, eyeing his very oblong balding head.

"Or else I'm just going to have to shave my head like you." My brother strokes his shiny scalp and patchy hair with a knuckly, liver-spotted hand.

"I highly recommend waxing instead," I joke. Whit responds with a chuckle that morphs into a more penetrating look of alarm.

"Wisty, I will *so* kill you if you can't change us back."

"Lighten up. We've always been able to revert, right? Not always at the most convenient moment, of course, but the spells never last forever."

At least I hope not.

Chapter 73

Whit

WISTY AND I ARE CLOSE enough now to hear what these citizens are chanting about, and it's pretty vile.

"Books equal chaos! We want order! Books equal chaos!"

We wander/hobble into the crowd and gradually nudge our way forward to a spot where we can see what's going on.

"Books equal chaos! We want order! Books equal chaos!"

Who are *these people who've been utterly convinced that books lead only to chaos, fear, evil?*

The scary thing is, they look normal. I suppose they *are* normal. At least, in their own minds. They probably wake up and have a cup of coffee and feed their whiny kids and hug their families. I spot a couple of the grown-ups here with a toddler on their shoulders; there with a baby in a backpack.

But there's something different and creepy about them, too. There's something missing from their eyes. They're alive, they're living, but there's not much *spark of life* or real passion.

The imposing stone building behind the park has a set of stairs leading up to its colonnaded entryway and is flanked on either side by two stone lions. The inscribed name over the enormous filigreed doors has been blasted away, but it's plain that this was at some point a big city library.

Judging from the pile of books out front, it's currently empty enough for a soccer match or a mega–rock concert. The pile is taller than the top of a goalpost.

And right now it's being doused with kerosene by a bunch of jackbooted New Order officials. A boiler-bellied man at the top of the steps is speaking into a megaphone and holding a torch above his head.

I don't know what it is about the New Order and their policy of hiring the most obscene-looking adults they can find, but they don't seem to be at risk of being understaffed. Take the meanest vice principal you've ever met, cross him with a praying mantis, and add in a tendency to bark like a German shepherd, and maybe you'll start to get close to what this N.O. guy is like.

"In the name of The One Who Is The One!" he yells. The crowd goes wild at this gibberish.

"In reparation for all those who have been lost forever to the wandering of the imagination! Lost to the obscene lust for dreams... and to knowledge for knowledge's sake!"

My "elderly" ears are about ready to shatter with the roar of the crowd, and I have to plug them.

"As punishment against those who have squandered their duty to Order and Society by indulging in the wastefulness, inefficiency, and lack of productivity that these cursed volumes engender!"

Wisty can't take it either. She slips up and gives me a look of complete disgust.

"And as a warning to all who stand here today as *imposters*" — I swear he's looking straight at us now — "those of you pretenders who do not *truly* believe in everything that the Order has done to transform us and provide for the stability of our future, *you shall burn, too.* We will *find* you, and you will *burn!*"

The crowd noise is earsplitting now. "Burn! Burn! Burn!" they chant. I think one of my half-deaf eardrums actually pops.

Wisty tries to make up for her slip and chants along with them. "Burn! Burn! Burn! Burn those crummy old books!"

I say a prayer that my sister doesn't *accidentally* make herself light up.

"Let us begin our ritual to cleanse our town, our community, our lives, of these germs and aberrations. We shall count down from five, and then we shall be free! *Five!*"

The crowd joins in. *"Four! Three! Two!"* The ground trembles underneath their foot-stomping. *"One!"*

And now the torch is arcing, end over end, through the air toward the kerosene-doused stack of books, thousands of books, many of which I recognize by their covers.

I tense up and dispatch all of my concentration and energy toward the torch. It takes more effort than I would have thought. But then the torch stops in midair, hovers, and then zooms straight back at the potbellied official. To my utter delight, his hair catches fire.

The crowd quickly goes silent, but we're not done yet. I see Wisty staring at the book pile. And she closes her eyes and mutters something—I get only a brief snippet of it: something about *kissing joy as it flies*—and then the books' pages start heaving up and down. Almost as if they're breathing...alive.

The covers start flapping...like wings.

They're flying! The books are *flying!*

They cascade up into the sky with a glorious rustling sound, like a thousand birds singing with new energy and life. They drift into the form of an enormous V, as you would see geese or swans doing, only of course there are tens of thousands of book-birds in this flock.

And then these escaped prisoners—having narrowly dodged execution—start winging toward the setting sun, to the west. Just like us.

"They're a protected species in Freeland," says Wisty.

Chapter 74

A GEYSER OF FLUTTERING shapes erupts out of the city ahead of Byron Swain and momentarily casts a shadow over him and his team of N.O. killers. Though calling them a "team" is being too kind, or at the least is imprecise.

They had certainly been brainwashed to kill the person they had smelled on the broken drumstick that had been thrust into their cages. They were definitely powerful and fast. They had teeth designed for tearing through raw flesh, and they had long, untrimmed fingernails that looked and sliced like claws.

And they were just kids. Once *human* kids. Byron isn't quite sure what they are now. Only that they are the best of the best at one thing: killing other kids.

He is certain that any one of them could take apart a full-grown adult in a single pounce. A whole pack of them set loose on one victim is utterly gratuitous, and The One knows it. *It is as if he wants Wisty to be brought back in as many pieces as possible,* Byron thinks bitterly.

His feral soldiers are always hungry and easily distracted by anything that moves—i.e., potential food. So when the strange flock of boxlike birds sweeps toward the horizon, the little freaks take off running.

"What the...?" Byron wonders, trying to make sense of the enormous cloud forming over the city.

Not birds, but...books? *Flapping books?*

There is only one explanation for such an outrageous sight. The One has the power to do it, but he would never set an entire library free.

Only Wisteria Allgood can. And she would, too.

"They're close," he whispers. At first his

heart leaps at the thought. He can save her—
it's what he is meant to do.

And then it crashes again. There is no *point*
in saving Wisty, really.

"They're close!" he yells, this time to his
crew, pointing ahead toward the majestic
plume in the sky. *"Find her!"*

There is no hope for him or for this world,
he knows—indeed, he knows so much more
than the rest of the innocents in Freeland. So
he will proceed with his plan.

Byron Swain and Wisteria Allgood will both
die—together—at the hands and teeth of his
own feral soldiers.

Byron hangs back a bit farther than usual.
The young killers probably aren't intelligent or
experienced enough to notice, but he doesn't
want them to see him cry.

It's just that...his heart aches so much.

Chapter 75

Whit

ONE THING WISTY AND I learn about looking and feeling old is that it's not only inconvenient but really problematic for prison escapees like us.

"What is *up* with this? I feel like I'm about ready to have a heart attack just from walking up this hill," I pant when we get a few miles outside the town where we liberated the books. "Don't tell me I'm gonna be *this* out of shape at age sixty-five. When will this spell wear off?"

"You're already sounding like a grumpy old fart, Whit. If you can't hack it, we can try some more sp—" Wisty breaks off when she's interrupted by the world's most terrifying screech.

And I do mean *screech.* A high-pitched, frenetic wail of something that I can describe only as murderous delight.

And they haven't even begun *the murdering part yet,* I realize as I turn my head and see a swarm of hunched shapes scampering madly after us at an incredible speed. It's pathetic that the millions of dollars spent on sports-car design seemingly can't duplicate nature's design for the insane charge of starving animals eyeing their prey.

"Run!" I grab Wisty's arm, and we run—if you can call it running, that is.

You see, running just isn't the same when you're a senior citizen. *There's no way we can outpace these things,* I'm thinking. *They're like greyhounds from hell.*

"Oh my God, *Whit!"* Wisty gasps as she realizes that our magic, which saved us in the last town, may actually end up being the death of us now.

The fearsome creatures let loose a terrifying group howl, and an electric shiver runs up my spine. I drag Wisty under an overpass and duck off the road, out of sight behind the rampart, but I know the creatures will be able to smell us at any moment.

"Okay, Wisty, I've got an idea." I actually don't have one. But I've got to figure something out this time. My sister's way too freaked to focus her powers right now.

I peek around the rampart and see that the...strangely shaped humans? baboons?... are still a good quarter mile away. I also spot a figure gliding along behind them on one of those two-wheeled electric scooter things.

I recognize the stiff-backed, pompous posture immediately, even at this distance. "Byron!"

"What?" Wisty spits out in disbelief. "You've got to be kidding me."

"He's behind this!" I hiss.

"Whit, you don't know that. Last time we saw him, he saved us!"

"Correction: last time we saw him, he flushed us down the toilet."

"But maybe he can help—"

"Wisty, we don't have time to play guessing games. Okay?"

The howling is uncomfortably near, and I

press Wisty hard against the wall of the over-pass so we're as flat and as far out of sight as possible. "Listen to me. We're going to turn ourselves into birds. That's our only hope. I can't do it alone, but we can probably do it to—"

And that is as much as I get out of my mouth before the wall where we are hiding falls away. Wisty and I collapse with it, and everything goes mostly dark.

Chapter 76

Whit

NEVER IN OUR ENDLESS days of fighting in the Overworld have Wisty and I *accidentally* fallen through a portal. I mean, usually they come and go, and when you get in, sometimes it's like being sucked into an F5 tornado. And you can't always be entirely sure where you'll end up.

But this time, I know exactly where we are the second we get through the passageway. I know it from the cold. As if it's coming from my own bones. In the Shadowland, you feel the chill deep *inside* you even before you feel it on your skin. That's just one of the place's many charms.

The next thing I notice is that we've returned

to our regular teenage bodies. *Maybe it's hard for a spell to hold through different dimensions?*

In *this* dimension, all we can see is gray, all we can feel is the glass-hard ground, all we can hear for a few minutes is our own breathing.

"God, I'm soooo cold," Wisty says when she realizes where we are. "This is taking me right back to my death-row stint in The One's cheery little snow globe at the BNW."

"Better cold than getting dismembered by Lost Ones," I say, looking around for any sign of the foul creatures.

"Oh, you can't fool me for a second, Whitford Allgood," Wisty says. "You're *happy* to be here." There she goes, reading my mind again. And, yeah, in case you're wondering, I *have* already been thinking about Celia, and if she's close by.

No. I'm not thinking about her...I'm *feeling* her.

She's near. There's a scent that gives me a strange kind of buzz, and a magnetic sort of pull that begins somewhere in my solar plexus. I start breathing faster and take a few steps in the direction where I feel her drawing me to her.

"You swear you didn't mean for us to end up here, Whit?" Wisty asks. "Be honest."

I don't answer her, because just then I hear a voice. The voice I dream of day and night. Not specific words, but the music and rhythm of it, drifting from the fog like the sounds of harps and wind chimes.

"Celia?" I call out, turning in every direction. There it is again. I can find it. I know I can get to her if I move fast enough and follow my instincts....

But part of the Shadowland's being an utterly featureless, cold, gray wasteland includes not having a whole lot of useful landmarks—and so, after just a few paces in the direction of the sound, a hand clutches my arm hard enough to crush bone. I whirl around, ready to fight a Lost One to the death, if that's even possible.

"Whitford Allgood!" It's Wisty, and her eyes are bulging with alarm. "You were just about to run off without me! What in God's name are you *thinking?*"

"I'm thinking that Celia can help us. She helped us before." I remind her of our first big prison break ages ago. But Wisty rolls her eyes and looks at me like an annoyed parent.

"Whit, can you just focus on *us* for a second and forget about your *totally dead* girlfriend?" Not too long ago, I would have yelled at her for a comment like that. "And, like, maybe how we're going to get out of here without becoming Lost Ones ourselves?"

And, right then, as if to put an exclamation point on her sentence, we hear something horrific coming through the fog behind us. It's different than the pathetic moan of Lost Ones. This time, it's the unmistakable sound of murderous hunger.

Byron's creepy animals!

"They're *Curves?*" shouts Wisty.

"And they've found our portal!"

Chapter 77

Whit

SPRINTING THROUGH THE Shadow-land is like skiing downhill with your eyes closed. Pure terror. Our hungry and relentless pursuers might be equally screwed by how easy it is to get lost in this formless landscape, but we're doubly doomed by their sense of smell, which I have no doubt can slice right through fog. Which means...

My sister and I are about to be torn apart and devoured on the cold ground of the Shadowland.

A low moaning cuts through the mist a stone's throw ahead. For a second I'm confused and think that somehow we've gone in a circle and the weird creatures are in front of us now, ready to pounce and start devouring.

But I'm wrong.

"Lost Ones!" yells Wisty.

And then there they are—their ragged shadows, the glinting light of their eye slits. And there are *so many* of them—dozens of the ghouls converging on us.

"This way," I tell Wisty. "As soon as we see the yellows of their eyes, we're going to the left—*hard* left."

"I just hope it doesn't put us right back into the mouths of those *other* killers!"

"Me, too. Left, then right. Stay on my back."

The Lost Ones are looming up and fanning out as we get close, but we're not yet close enough. "Not yet, not yet, not yet," I tell Wisty.

And I brace myself for their cold. Fifteen yards, ten yards, five yards—there it is! The cold hits us like a ton of ice.

"Now!" I yell, and wheel left, my hand holding Wisty's behind me. *She's* got *to keep*

up. One, two, three, four, five, six, seven—
"Back right!"

And then, behind us, the moaning suddenly meets the howling and it's as if there's a battle royal going on between all the mummies and werewolves ever conceived.

"It worked!" I yell. "So far anyway. Keep watching for them—*everywhere.*"

And then more happens in the next five seconds than has happened in any other moment of my life, or probably anyone else's.

We hear Byron scream out, "Call them off, you idiot!"

"You call off yours!" replies a female voice, one that makes my heart race and then go cold in the next beat.

"There's a portal!" yells Wisty, pointing at the telltale fog swirl ahead.

"That was *Celia's* voice!" I gasp, stopping in my tracks.

"Don't you *dare*," my sister snaps.

And then, though I have ninety pounds on her and a whole lot more muscle and sports experience than she does, my little sister hits me with a flying tackle that takes me out at the knees and drives me straight through the portal.

Okay…it's not *quite* that simple. It never is.

Chapter 78

Whit

I DON'T KNOW *where* I am exactly, but somehow I'm not too worried about it. I'm with *Celia,* and that's all that matters for the moment.

"I had the weirdest dream about you," I tell her. "I was running from dozens of Lost Ones—"

"We only have a short time together," interrupts Celia. "Let's not waste it."

She presses her head against my chest, and I'm sure she can hear my heart beating. I've missed her so much, so badly, constantly. The only weird thing is, for some reason she put on too much of her perfume. I mean, I love the smell of it, but it's so strong right now I keep fighting back sneezes and my eyes are stinging.

"I love you," I whisper urgently. "I missed you so much."

"We only have a short time together," she says. "Let's not waste it."

Didn't she just say that? Ah, who cares? We hug, and it feels as if we're merging into one again. I love that—it's incredible. Her presence and mine joining together like two clouds intermingling in a sunny sky.

"Have you ever felt this amazing?" I ask. "I haven't."

"We only have a short time together," she says. "Let's not waste it."

What the—? Hey, wait a second, is this a dream? Oh no, there's something wrong with her face! Is that—? Oh God...oh no!

Chapter 79

Wisty

AN AWFULLY LOUD NOISE WAKES me from an almost deathly slumber. I shoot up with a start—and a modest burst of flame. *Where am I? Somewhere outside... looks vaguely familiar...*

I stumble through the starlit darkness and barely manage to grab a railing. *Oh yeah. Okay.* I'm on the parapet of an abandoned factory my brother and I found after the portal ejected us into the rubble-strewn borderlands of Freeland.

And I was *supposedly* on night watch for three hours while poor Whit got some rest.

Down below there's some sort of scuffling. *Panting? Grunting? Oh no! I have to get Whit!*

But before I can even make it to the rooftop door, he's bursting through it.

"Byron and his freaks," he gasps. "They must have made it through the portal, too. They'll follow our scent up here. Is there another way down?"

I shake my head. "So we'll have to use magic, or fight—"

"There will be no fight," I hear Byron Swain declare haughtily as he casually slips through the door, shutting it behind him. His usual perfect timing.

We hear a rumbling of bodies trampling up the stairwell and pounding against the door frenetically. Byron's got a Command Pipe, and he plays several bold notes, which seems to settle the monsters down. But that doesn't stop Whit from pinning Byron's back against the door.

"We are *not* going anywhere without a fight, Swain," my brother says through gritted teeth. "There were a few minutes back at the BNW where I thought you were actually trying to help us. The toilet flush? That one could have gone either way. But then you show up with a pack of mad apes? You're not interested in saving us. You're interested in saving yourself."

"I'm very sad about this," says Byron, staring straight at me, and I'll admit that it looks as if he's fighting back tears. "To be perfectly honest, you're partially correct, but that's only a recent development. My Kill Team"—he nods sideways toward the beasts behind the door—"were to be the instrument of my own death, as well as yours." He sighs deeply, as if the weight of all this is too much to bear.

And the weirdest thing is, I'm starting to feel it, too. Normally I'd be ready to light up after hearing about his little assassination agenda—but now, his burden, his misery, his...well, his feelings for me, whatever they are...just kind of sock me in the gut and take my breath away. Instead of being scared and angry, I actually feel sorry for him.

"The only one who'll be dead is you," Whit spits.

"Shut up, Whit," I say. I turn back to the weasel. "B., are you looking me in the eye and saying that you intended this night to end with a suicide-murder massacre? Are you really that insane? I'd actually started to believe in you back at the BNW," I confess.

I think I see a flicker of hope in Byron's eyes, but it quickly turns dark. "Insane? I don't know, Wisty. I don't know what I am. Remember when I said that no one being exposed to The One's evil for a long time can remain unchanged? I've seen things in him, know things about him—*and* his victims—that have driven me to these lengths. I can't apologize for it. And...I can say without reservation, your life is better ending now than being forced to be with him. *Which is what he wants—and what he will get.*"

Okay. He has both my and Whit's attention now. Whit loosens his grip, but his tone is still harsh. "You have no belief in Freeland, then. In the Resistance. Or in us." Whit's eyes flare with so much bitterness that I think maybe *he* will light up.

"Oh, but I do," Byron says, finally unlocking his eyes from mine and looking at Whit. "Even you, jockstrap. I've been reading your journal. Very interesting stuff. Had no idea about *your* special Gift."

Whit looks surprised. "For writing, you mean?"

Byron snorts. "Are you kidding me? Most of that writing's straight from Ms. Magruder's class. And the stuff that isn't is—well, let's face it—utter dreck." The guy really has no fear of the fact that my brother can deck him, does he? "Do you mean to tell me you have no idea of your Gift?"

"First of all, Byron, I told you to quit talking like that," I jump in. It's obviously going to take a woman to move this conversation forward. "Second, just tell us what you're getting at. *Please?*"

"The evidence is there with a little interpolation," Byron continues in his stiff, blustery tone, "but I'm fairly convinced that Whit is clairvoyant."

Chapter 80

Whit

I WANT PROOF.

Because I know I've written some pretty grim things in my journal.

Including, but not limited to, the death of my sister.

"Would you care to," I sneer, "interpolate that statement for us?"

"That doesn't even make any sense." Byron looks annoyed. "I suppose you weren't *always* listening in Ms. Magruder's class. But, for starters, perhaps you'd like to explain to Wisty how you knew that the little Bionic Drummer Boy was going to get his arms...amputated."

My stomach curdles, and Wisty looks at me in shock as the weasel continues. "And it's also apparent that you know The One is going to bomb every inch of Freeland very soon. There are plenty of examples, but I suggest we save the rest of this fascinating discussion for better times."

I hear some disturbing growling start up outside the door, and Byron swiftly blows a few strong notes on his Command Pipe, which results in instant chill.

"Look, we know you're full of it, Swain, so let's move on to plan B."

"Yeah," Wisty jumps in. "Can't we agree to a nice, simple plan that doesn't end in a suicide pact?"

"And how about we start with you giving me back my *journal?*"

"You're in luck, Whit, because that's actually a part of my *new* plan." He turns his full attention back to Wisty. I'm continually stunned by the intense looks he throws her. Like she's his...Celia.

Wow. Scary thought. I instinctively put my arm around Wisty, as if that's going to protect her from his lustful eyes.

"Wisty, you and I both know that we could

do great things together," he says to her, and I tighten my grip on her shoulder. "You felt it onstage at Stockwood. You felt it when we made magic at the BNW. And your first *major* transformation was done on me, wasn't it? In case you forgot, it wasn't a weasel. Originally, you turned me into a *lion*. It was...electric."

Wisty is speechless. Her stomach has to be cramping way worse than mine now.

"I know you don't care all that much for me," he continues in the understatement of the century. "But you and I are so much *more* powerful together than you and your brother. The fact is, Wisty, I believe that *you and I* could actually be the two children of the prophecies."

"The prophecies say a *brother* and *sister!*" she spits out indignantly.

"The brother-sister detail is a technicality. I know you don't want to admit this, but you and Whit haven't yet executed the level of magic that Freeland needs in order to defeat The One. But when your energy goes through me, it becomes greater."

"Prove it!" Wisty demands.

"You've been blind to how much I've been intertwined with your life, your magic. You didn't even realize I was there when you turned everyone in Unger's courtroom into horseflies. And remember who allowed you two to take your drumstick and your journal when you were captured by the New Order?"

We're numb, speechless, confused, trying to process all of this.

Byron takes advantage of the moment, and as he strides away a few paces, we hear the growling behind the door stir up again. There are sharp scraping sounds—teeth or claws on metal?

Byron reaches for his Command Pipe but then suddenly drops it before he makes a sound.

"You have two options right now, Allgoods: We three can quickly end this hopeless quest as martyrs at the hands of the Kill Team. Or"—he lets us listen as the clamoring of hungry beasts gets more frenzied—"we take Whit to The One instead of Wisty. I believe he would accept *your* incredible Gift, Whit, instead of Wisty's."

"You don't know that he would," I say. "You don't even know that I have any Gift to... fortune-tell." I have to admit, I'm processing that one. "What about Wisty?"

"Wisty and I... well, together we can lead Freeland to victory." I snort loudly, but he turns earnestly to Wisty. "I *know* it, Wisty! I have what you need... in so many ways."

"No!" Wisty screams. "That's sick. I'm never leaving Whit."

Byron levels his gaze, increasingly focused and confident, at me. "Let's just let your brother decide that."

"What do you think I'm gonna say, Weasel?" I scoff. "We have other options that you don't know about." I'm looking at Wisty as if to say, *Don't we?*

"But the latter option is the only one that *Celia* would approve of."

Oh my God. He knows? How much does he know?

"She told you to turn yourself in, didn't she, Whit? For the greater good? So you could be together again?"

It's in my journal. He's a real bastard, but

he's right. In my head I can hear her saying it, I *feel* her commanding me: *Stop thinking about only what's right in front of you. Think about the rest of the lost.*

"It's what was meant to be, Whit. Accept your fate." Byron raises the Command Pipe to his lips. "Wisty, can I have your decision? My friends outside are very, very hungry."

"No! No, no, no!" Wisty shouts furiously, but she shoots me a look and I think I can read it. She has a plan, and I'm pretty sure I know what it is. Maybe I *can* see into the future.

"Whit?" Byron asks.

"No," I reply firmly. "Not a chance."

"Well, then," Byron responds with resignation, "we're finished here."

And then he sends out a command from his pipe—and the heavy rooftop door literally comes flying off its hinges.

Chapter 81

Wisty

THE SWARM OF BODIES, the claws and teeth, the screeches and growls, the stink and heat of their breath — it's everywhere. It's overwhelming, sickening. But I've never been more focused in my life.

The second that Byron blows the Command Pipe, I leap at him and it's as if we're two magnets. I'm on him — girl to boy — and I rip the pipe from his hands.

I'm surprised at how it slips easily out of his grip and into mine — but I'm one-tenth of a second too late.

I can already feel claws piercing the skin on my thighs.

There's a moment where I think my life is

going to end just the way Byron wanted it to. With me on top of him, clutching him for dear life, his raucous monsters taking both of us down at once. I don't like the image one bit.

But my focus is back, and I no longer feel too much of the pain of whatever mutilation has already started on my back and legs. I close my eyes and hum the notes into the Command Pipe, the very same ones Byron used earlier to subdue his brutes.

Perfect pitch has never been more perfect. Over and over I send out the command until I have enough courage to let myself absorb what's going on.

The beastly strikes have stopped. All I feel now is the pounding of Byron's raging heart. He's alive. I'm alive. And Whit?

Continuing with the series of notes, I open my eyes and roll off Byron. Whit's just a few feet away, on top of the monster that had gotten to me a few seconds before. He actually has the beast in a stranglehold. My brother really is something else.

There's thick, gloppy blood on me, on Byron, on the floor, on Whit. But what freaks me out more than anything else is what the creatures really look like. This is the first time we're seeing them up close.

They're *kids*. They're human children. What has the New Order *done* to them?

I'm surging with energy and righteous anger and power. Looking up at the sky, and then at Whit, *I transform us into birds*. Really fast ones. In a heartbeat, we're supersonic hummingbirds disappearing into the sky. The Command Pipe I'd been holding sails down toward the rooftop.

Far below, the last thing I see is the feral children descending on Byron.

I turn my head away. *I can't watch this.*

Chapter 82

Wisty

THE DOWNSIDE OF CHANGING yourself into any flying creature is that you just might be a couple of hundred feet up in the air when your spell wears off. Fortunately the unfortunate happened when we were only a dozen or so feet off the ground, dipping down toward our final destination: the entry to Garfunkel's.

We're greeted on the ground floor of the department store with deeply pained faces. Something really bad has been going down here, I can feel it. When Whit comes back from a near-death adventure without being greeted by cheers and Janine throwing herself at him, you know something's wrong.

At least Emmet's got his arms around me before we can even say, "Hey."

"I can't believe you're alive!" he chokes out, uncharacteristically emo.

"Since when do I make a habit of dying?" I try a bad joke.

"But it's been . . . *months!*" He absently runs his fingers through my now-longer hair, as if to emphasize the point. "What happened to you guys?"

Whit and I look at each other, thoroughly confused about the timing for a moment. "*The portal?*" he guesses, referring to the mysterious time-warp quality of some portals.

I look around at the group and nod at Whit. Yes, more than just a few weeks have passed. Definitely. It's almost as if everyone's gone pale somehow. More unkempt, slouched. They all have sunken cheeks and eyes. Emmet looks as if he should be holding a tin can and asking for loose change.

"Where's Janine?" Whit sounds alarmed.

"Back in Ladies' Shoes. Running therapy sessions for some of the messed-up kids. Jamilla's back there, too. But she's a patient instead of the doctor this time. It's been hard around here, guys," he reports grimly.

"Let's head to Accessories and get caught up," Whit says to us.

"Why's it so *dark?*" I ask as we move toward the back of the store.

"Brownout," Emmet explains. "Too many bombs, every day, all day and night."

Sasha's back in Accessories strumming a particularly gloomy tune on his guitar. As he comes over to greet us, I notice that the zealot's confidence is gone from his stride. In the next few minutes, the stories he and Emmet tell make it pretty clear why.

The past month saw the beginning of the next stage in the New Order's plan for domination. The first wave of kids who were kidnapped and reprogrammed in facilities — those that weren't vaporized anyway — were just then being released back into society so that their little 'bot brains could take root and flourish. Meanwhile, a second wave of intensive kidnappings began, and the New Order's scout teams probed deep into Freeland. At least a dozen kids from Garfunkel's had been captured when they were out on food-collection missions, including some of the kids we'd already saved once from other facilities.

Talk about three steps forward and one huge, megastep back.

We've lost our homes, friends, families — an entire world. And now we're losing one another.

Chapter 83

Whit

JANINE MEETS UP with us on our way to Ladies' Shoes—and I think she's changed more than anyone else here. She's thinner, which might have made her face even prettier, but she's gotten harder and tougher, too.

She spots me, and though she's definitely stressed, she greets me with a smile. "Whit, you're finally back." She glances at Wisty and just says her name. I'm not used to this kind of weak reception, and it hurts, but I don't show anything. Everyone here has been through a lot.

"Hi, Janine. It's good to see you. Really good," I say, and leave it at that.

"I take it Sasha and Emmet brought you up

to speed? It's scary out there, guys. The New Order's turned some kids…*bestial*," she explains.

"They're monsters." I nod. "We've met them."

"Good, then you and Wisty can probably help. If you're planning on staying around, that is." I guess I'm not exactly what you'd call a reliable constant in Janine's life. "Help us get everyone moving, okay? Tell them what they can expect. Try not to scare them too much." She looks over at her traumatized crew of kids. "How's your magic? Your Gifts?"

"On and off," I say. "We flew here, but then we crash-landed."

"Well, let's hope you're more *on* than off today. We have to get out of this place, like, *now*. It was nice living in a department store while it lasted," she says, looking around at the disheveled place the Freelanders had called home for so many months. Months that felt like an eternity.

Then Janine starts to clap her hands loudly and shout out orders. "We know from intelligence that the New Order is coming *tonight, everyone.* We have to get everyone out, and I mean everyone, even the sick and wounded. Let's move it, everybody! We have a plan for evacuating. Let's execute it perfectly."

She stops for a breath and makes eye contact with me. "It's good to see you, Whit. You look older. It suits you."

Janine seems older, too—and it suits her.

Chapter 84

Whit

NOW THAT GARFUNKEL'S HAS BEEN seriously breached, we need to move to a new protected location, but no one's sure exactly where. Janine, Sasha, Emmet, Wisty, and I debate the options as we hike through the tunnel underneath the once-famous department store that used to sponsor football games and the holiday parade.

"Within hours Freeland is going to be blanketed with bombs or totally teeming with New Order patrols. Or both." I recount the details of what Byron had told me and Wisty at the factory. "We're going to have to go back across the border into New Order territory. Maybe just lie low and wait it out."

"But where?" Janine asks. "We've been living out of Garfunkel's for so long we don't really know what's going on out there. That's the problem with getting too comfortable."

"How about the Stockwood reservoir?" Sasha suggests.

"Too risky," I say. "The Bionics know about it, and we know they were working for The One." I glance at Wisty's pained face. "Most of them anyway."

"How about the abandoned Electio factory, Whit?" Janine says.

"Breached by the enemy," Sasha replies.

Wisty suggests the City of Progress. "They won't bomb there, and maybe Mrs. Highsmith can help with the sick and wounded."

After some discussion, we decide that's the best plan we have. We'll try to do a group transformation when we get closer—to disguise ourselves as a rally, or a parade of Sector Leader's Stars of Honor. The old tunnels don't run all the way there, though, so we're faced with having to do the last piece of the journey aboveground and without a vehicle.

"Maybe there's a portal that will get us there," I suggest.

"Right. Let's go hang out in the Shadowland," scoffs Wisty. "They're always rolling out the red carpet for us. Especially when they're hungry."

"We're all exhausted," Janine says. "We've been walking for hours, and a lot of us haven't slept in at least a day. Let's get a few hours' rest before we make our break into the open."

And that's right about when the bombing begins. And it's the worst ever.

With the tunnel shaking like a jackhammer, and without our knowing whether or not this tube is strong enough to withstand the blasts, no one is getting much rest—let alone *sleep*. Instead we huddle together quietly and tightly—not for warmth but for safety.

Janine and I, leaning our backs against the wall, rest together. Wisty has her head in Emmet's lap. Sasha is cradling his guitar. The rest of the kids are in a tangle around us.

We're just waiting here to die, aren't we?

Chapter 85

Wisty

WHIT AND I CHANCE a peek outside. The sun is high in a perfectly blue sky by the time the N.O. artillery has quieted down. We can see the City of Progress skyline a few miles away, across bombed-out Freeland. *Now what?*

Since none of us got much sleep, and miles of trekking ahead of us meant we'd need as much energy as possible, Whit and I had worked hard to conjure up a breakfast buffet for the entire group — complete with bacon, eggs, and waffles. This was a feast way bigger than Whit's earlier soup-kitchen trick. Realizing that maybe we'd never have to survive solely on Garfunkel's Cashew Crunch again was a definite breakthrough for us and our powers.

Here's how we did it: taking a cue from what Whit and I learned at the BNW Center, we'd practiced doing our magic *with* the group, holding hands, and it worked like a dream. I'd even started taking stock in Byron's wild theories about our magic becoming greater when it passes through others. This *could* be the secret to our success....

Of course, waffles help a whole lot, too. We've been living in a tunnel for half a day, so sun plus breakfast equals a group of kids who are now officially sunny-side up.

And it's a good thing, because it's not that long before we spot a ponderous black V formation of at least fifty N.O. bombers creeping right toward us. This is the battle we've been waiting for, and we'd rehearsed our plan. To the extent that you can actually "rehearse" defeating a world-dominating enemy.

So that's how it came to pass that rather than hiding in rubble, we're now standing boldly in the barren landscape and staring hard at the planes speeding toward us.

"You ready?" Emmet shouts above the squadron roar. He flashes me a confident smile, and I nod.

"Okay, people, *focus, focus, focus!*" I shout out like I'm a gym teacher running a tough calisthenics regimen. "Wait until they're almost right overhead but not directly enough to bomb us. I'll tell you when!"

And, at what I hope is precisely the right moment, Whit and I begin to conduct a chorus of voices.

> *"Be that word our sign of parting, bird or*
> *fiend!…*
> *Get thee back into the tempest and the Night's*
> *Plutonian shore!*
> *Leave no black plume as a token of that lie*
> *thy soul hath spoken!*
> *Leave my loneliness unbroken!"*

And suddenly the breath's gone out of me, and some of the others actually collapse to the ground from the effort, or the power surge, or whatever it is that's happening....

Because, to be honest, we're not exactly sure what's going on.

The planes definitely start tipping, then spiraling downward. The wings seem to be... missing?

"They're going to crash!" someone cries out. "Into us!"

"Again!" I scream. "We need to say the words again! Everybody together!"

The bombers are careening sideways toward us, and we don't have the energy left to find cover — not that there's any cover in this flattened wasteland. A bunch of us manage to clasp our hands together and recite the spell all over again.

The bombers are now grotesquely distorted. They're, like, half machine, half creature. And they're still coming for us.

"Look straight at them!" I yell. "And let's chant one more time!"

One *last* time, that is, because if this doesn't work, right now, we're all roadkill.

There's a plane fewer than a hundred yards

from flattening me, and I close my eyes as I say the last line.

When I open them, I'm ravenously hungry. *I see nothing in the sky* . . . except a whole bunch of wheeling ravens. Apparently we just turned their bombers into birds.

Chapter 86

Wisty

IT'S TOTALLY, TOTALLY mindblowing. That was a real military battle, wasn't it? We're unarmed. And we won? A bunch of kids beat the N.O.?

The thrill of victory is followed by another and yet another success. We've seriously upped the Freeland raven population, *and* our confidence is sky-high.

We're clearly running on adrenaline for a while as we triumph through several similar battles. Eventually, though, we're running on empty. The magic has consumed every calorie from that bacon-and-waffle breakfast. Everyone's basically curled up on the ground, trying to recoup some steam.

"Another squadron on the way!" Sasha suddenly shouts, pointing into the distance. I think that if I ask them to join hands one more time, everybody is going to start crying. Even bouncy Emmet has dark bags under his eyes. "Wisty," he says, "shouldn't we come up with another plan?"

My eyes follow the planes. "They're not coming our way. They're veering off toward—"

"Where we came from," finishes Whit with a shudder. "Garfunkel's."

We don't know if someone got their intel messed up on the New Order side, but they must think we're still there. Because they proceed to drop what seems like their entire N.O. arsenal on the center of the town behind us. Right where Garfunkel's is.

Or *was*.

Where some of the Resistance kids were still hiding out, after refusing to leave with the rest of us. They'd thought our quest was a suicide mission.

I look at Whit, and he's squinting hard, obviously holding back tears. We watch as the store—and maybe even those kids—all go up in flames.

We're mesmerized by the twisted fireworks finale until Sasha calls out again. He's pointing toward the horizon—a horizon that's disappearing under a black cloud...that isn't a cloud at all. It's still *more* New Order planes.

And under the black cloud are gray curtains, the way you can sometimes see rain falling beneath a distant thundercloud. Only in this case it's not rain—*it's bombs.*

As they hit the ground, there are eye-stinging flashes of blue light. We can feel the earth shaking, even from however many miles away we are.

Is it the beginning of the end? Or just the end?

Chapter 87

Whit

"LET'S GET EVERYONE underground!" I shout to Wisty. "I saw a manhole a while back. Maybe we can hide there."

We manage to get the group to the manhole, and, as luck would have it, it's an old steam tunnel rather than a sewer. Not the freshest air in the world, but the tunnel should be far enough underground to make us safe from explosions and flying shrapnel.

Once everyone's in, Wisty pulls me aside.

"Unless you have any better ideas, I think you and I need to go to Mrs. Highsmith's," she tells me. "She's powerful. She might be able to..." I don't think she's even sure what the woman can do for us.

"Give us options?" I finish the thought.

"Exactly." Wisty nods. "Maybe even give us info about Mom and Dad. I just have this feeling she knows where they are…"

Just then Janine walks up to us, her eyes still tinged with red from watching our longtime home bite the dust. "What's next, guys? Any bright ideas? Any dim ones?"

"Listen, Janine, we've got to go to Mrs. Highsmith," I tell her. Then I put my hands on her arms. "You okay here with the group?"

"Yes, but…" Janine looks down at her black combat boots. I think she's trying to hide that she's getting choked up again.

I lift her chin gently and force her to look at me with those sage-green eyes.

"Why do I have this awful feeling that this is *it?* It's the last time I'm going to say good-bye to you, isn't it?" She speaks in a whispery voice. It sends a shiver rushing up my spine.

"The last time you're going to say good-bye, yeah," I acknowledge. "But not the last time you'll see me. I promise."

She can't help the tears from spilling out of her eyes. My hands cup her face, and I wipe the streams away with my thumbs. Her hands slide down my arms to my wrists, as if she doesn't want to let me go.

I'm not exactly sure what I feel for Janine. But I do know what I have to do right now.

So I kiss her sweetly. Long enough to tell her everything without words — some crazy, mixed-up jumble of admiration, appreciation, attraction. I feel all of those things for her right now. Deeply.

I don't stop kissing her until Wisty's finished saying her good-byes, and she tugs my shirt gently. "C'mon, Whit."

I let Janine go, and she just nods. There are no more good-byes as Wisty and I climb the metal rungs up the manhole shaft to the war zone above.

Chapter 88

Whit

"YOU'RE LATE," Mrs. Highsmith says through the intercom, buzzing open the building's front door even before we can press her button. *How did she know?*

"We didn't have an appointment, did we?" I ask Wisty, still mystified as we hurry up the stairs and find her apartment door open. And, in the kitchen, there's that little old ninja lady, definitely looking more poet than ninja as she stands over a massive oil barrel that's almost as tall as she is. She's stirring something that smells pretty rank. She takes a sip and totally gags on her own brew.

This is the lady who's going to be our game changer? Who can help save us?

"So we get to talk at last, Whitford. My crystal always revealed you to be a fairly good-looking young man, but now that I can get a nice, close-up view, I see you're what they call a 'hottie' these days."

Can I just confirm for you that it's *unbelievably* creepy to be ogled by an old witch? I shift uncomfortably from foot to foot.

"Except you could learn to stand up a bit straighter, dear. Adds inches. Now, how did you two find the trip, by the way?" she asks as if we've just taken a little jaunt to Grandma's house.

"Um, it was sort of...like, there's a *war* going on out there?" I offer weakly.

Wisty sums up the hellacious journey of the last three and a half hours. "Let's just say, Mrs. H., if you ever have the opportunity to sprint for your life ahead of a curtain of bombs that explode and burn so hot that the buildings and sidewalks and streets and the very dirt itself melt into glass...well, see what your other options are *and embrace them with all your being!*"

"Oh, I shall, Wisteria." She laughs. "These

old bones don't sprint anywhere anymore any-way." *Can this lady be serious?* "Yes," she says, looking at me as if to warn me she might be able to read my mind. "It showed some real chutzpah, making the decision to come here through all of that. Your parents are very proud of you."

"How do you know that?" Wisty blurts.

"Have you heard from them?" I ask at the same time.

"I *have.* And you are about to, my dears. I've been practicing my holographic technique and, wouldn't you know, your parents just popped up!"

Wisty and I look at each other. "Isn't that the same thing The One was talking about back at the BNW Center?" I exclaim, first with surprise, then with horror. For all we know, this strange little lady might be partners with the guy.

"But it's not... *real,* is it?" Wisty'd hoped that the twisted hallucination of our parents was just The One's theatrics.

"Oh, it's real, all right," Mrs. H. says, and I frown. *What does "real" mean anymore any-*

way? "Come here, and I'll show you. Come quickly. I don't know how long my magic will last."

We weave our way around the barrel and settle down at a table cluttered with stacks of books, pens, paper, candles, matches, and the odd pot and pan.

"Now, where did it disappear to? Oh, here we go." She lifts up a dirty dishcloth to reveal — as if she's just itching to make her whole witchy image complete — something that looks like a *glass ball.*

This can't be where the answers to our problems lie.

"How does it work?" Wisty asks.

"Ask your brother." Mrs. H. looks at me and smiles knowingly. "Here, Whit. Put your palm on the glass." She picks up my hand and places it on the ball along with hers. The globe feels really warm, like a coffee pot that's only just starting to cool down.

There's a flash of light as soon as my hand makes contact.

"Whoa!" I say. I definitely felt something surge from me — something powerful — but

I'm too freaked out to let on. I'm *so* not ready to accept this new gig as a fortune-teller.

"Ben? Liz? You still there?" Mrs. H. shouts as if she's yelling into a phone with a bad connection. "Your children decided to show up. I gather the bombings slowed them down a bit."

I can't believe what I'm seeing play out right under my hand. Clouds and shapes swirling and then coming together — as the faces of my parents suddenly appear.

"Mom! Dad!" Wisty and I shout together.

They still look eerily gaunt, but this time Dad's eyes are open, thank God, and they both smile when they hear our voices.

"Whit! I see you so clearly!" Mom says. "Can Wisty come a little closer? We need to talk."

Chapter 89

Whit

GREAT! WE'RE TRYING to fight a war, our parents are scheduled to be executed, and they're having a "we need to talk" moment. Here's the thing: you never grow up in your parents' eyes.

Wisty pushes me to the side a little. "I'm here. Mom! Dad! Are you okay? We're so worried about you," she says in a burst of words and emotion.

"Don't worry about us," Dad says firmly, avoiding Wisty's question. "We don't have much time, but we wanted to let you know how you're doing."

I'm more confused now than I was even a

second ago. "Shouldn't *we* be telling *you* how we're doing?'"

Mom shakes her head. "You've been so brave—both of you. We're very proud of your strength and spirit. It's been tough going, we know, but you're really getting the hang of the magic. And you're starting to understand how to share it, which is extremely important."

"The thing is," Dad jumps in, "time is starting to run a little bit short. So...we wanted to suggest that you...pick up the pace a bit."

"Dad! *Pick up the pace?*" Wisty's a little indignant now. Good old Dad, always trying to get us to be the first and the fastest.

"You may have to do some things that don't feel...right to you. Things outside of your comfort zone. Whit knows all about that, right, Whit? 'No pain, no gain.' You'll need to be counterintuitive at times."

Wisty looks troubled, but I can't help hearing Celia's voice in my head. "Do you mean, like...turning ourselves in?" I ask.

Wisty shakes her head and butts in. "But, Mom, we've had *so* much pain! We've got blood and scars all over ourselves to prove it."

Her voice is trembling now. "You're our parents! Don't you want us to be safe?"

"Doing important things isn't always safe, sweetie," Mom says with a pained look. "It's the hardest lesson for a parent to teach, or for some kids to learn. But that's what the Allgoods were born for. You've found your Gifts. Now give them away."

"Give them away?" I exclaim. "What's that mean? To who? *The One?*"

"That's insane!" Wisty shouts, and I'm instantly reminded of her wild ways back in school.

"I'm so sorry, sweetheart, but that's about all we can tell you right now," Dad says. "Because it's all we know. We love you and miss you both…"

Our parents' faces begin to fade. And they're both smiling bravely.

"Don't go yet! Mom! *Dad!*" Wisty is still shouting. *"Please don't go!"*

Mrs. Highsmith shushes her. "My neighbors cause me trouble enough without them complaining about somebody yelling in my kitchen," she says.

"But we need to talk to them some more," Wisty argues. "We really do."

Mrs. H. is already up and back at her freaking cauldron-thingy.

"The important thing is that your parents are safe for the moment, even if they're in a little trouble, shall we say."

"'A little trouble'? Listen, lady," I tell her, ignoring the fact that it's probably a bad idea to insult a crazy witch, "we risked our lives coming here to get *advice*. Our parents are on death row. Our friends are trapped in a steam pipe under a war zone. The New Order has nearly completed their total occupation of the Overworld. And we don't have any clues about what The One wants from Wisty or how we're supposed to win against these egomaniacal wackjobs."

She stops stirring her pot and looks at us, rather amused. It's enough to drive me insane when a grown-up does that. And they do it *all the time.*

"Heavens, children. The clues are all there in front of you. You just have to look harder. And as for what The One wants with your sister, well, it's perfectly obvious what you have, my dear, that *he* doesn't have."

It's the worst possible moment for a gale-force wind to crash through the apartment windows and virtually demolish the apartment. And us.

The One has found us!

"You told him we were here!" Wisty shouts at the old witch.

Chapter 90

Wisty

I'VE NEVER FELT his power as strongly as I do right now.

After barely escaping flying shards of glass, Whit and I are gripping an old-fashioned radiator, holding ourselves down and out of the way of crashing furniture, cutlery, and appliances as a tornado of fury tears through the apartment.

Mrs. Highsmith, on the other hand, resolutely stands her ground in the middle of the swirling maelstrom. "He's mastered the air!" she shouts through the din. "Study his every move. *Learn* from this."

It's been hard enough ducking flying toasters and pots with the floor steady under our feet. But now it gets ten times harder as the ground turns into something like gelatin. It's a bona fide earthquake, courtesy of The One. The rattling and crashing and tipping furniture ratchets up the decibel level to deafening, earsplitting. My head is pounding.

"And he's mastered the earth!" Mrs. Highsmith continues, hollering her lesson over the madness. The One seems to oblige by precisely illustrating her next point. "And he's mastered the water!"

Now it's raining—*inside the apartment*. The room is filling with churning water, quickly making its way up to our quivering knees.

"There's only one thing he needs to completely secure his present and future domination, and to complete himself. His ego is huge. That's his strength *and* his weakness. *Do you follow... MY DRIFT?*"

Then Mrs. Highsmith levitates into the air, presumably to avoid having to swim in her own kitchen, but judging from the look of terror-flecked anger on her face, I realize she's not doing it under her own control. In a second, she's pretty much pinned up against the ceiling, her face twisted in profound agony. Then her eyes begin to bulge unnaturally.

She's being crushed to death, isn't she?

"Liar!" she screams inexplicably, and suddenly the room goes still. "Show yourself!"

And then, as if an invisible pair of forceps has reached inside the apartment, she's yanked out of a broken window and into the howling wind outside, screaming, "Show yourself!" the whole way.

Chapter 91

Wisty

WE'RE DEAD QUIET, Whit and I. There is just not much to say after you witness something as strange and horrible as what just happened in Mrs. Highsmith's apartment.

But then Whit is ever practical. "Let's get out of here before The One *shows himself.* Or sends his soldiers."

Too late. Sort of.

We don't even have a chance to get to the door before I hear an eerie and familiar song drifting in through the broken window. Notes that have forever burned themselves into my memory.

The Command Pipe. The Command Pipe of Byron Swain, to be exact.

I go to the window, ignoring Whit's cry of "Wisty! No! Stay away from there!"

Down on the City of Progress's unblemished sidewalk is a depressingly familiar crowd of feral freaks led by—*quelle surprise*—Mr. Untrustworthy himself.

But you know what? I also feel a wave of relief—completely out of my control, I might add—that Byron is alive. Go figure.

Whit's standing behind me protectively, then he leaps to the apartment entry to start barricading the door, just in case this ends in, you know, a little reprise of our last encounter with B. and his toothy, drooling friends.

"So, Wisty, I guess you didn't figure it all out yet," Byron says with little emotion. "If you'd done the right thing—if you'd been listening to what we've all been telling you—I might be able to help you right now. But you didn't. So I can't."

A note of anger enters his voice, and he glares at Whit, who's back by my side. "So now I'm afraid I have to do what *Celia* told me to do."

"What are you talking about, Swain?" yells Whit. "Don't you dare talk about Celia."

"When I chased you into the Shadowland, I met up with your old girlfriend. To be more exact, her people met up with my people." I remember the moment, and I know Whit does, too. "And I regret to inform you, lover boy, she's a Lost One now. She and her new friends were about to *consume* us—and that means she'd eat you, too."

I don't even need to look at Whit to feel the energy radiating off his body: he wants to launch himself out the window at Byron. "But that's impossible!" he screams.

"What's *wrong* with you, Byron?" I yell. "You act like you care about me, and then you lie, and threaten, and betray me every time we meet—"

"*Lie?* Wisty, tell me one good reason why I should lie. Tell me what I have to live for now."

I have to admit, I can't answer that one. Never could. Not even when Byron was in preschool with me.

"Prove to me that you spoke to Celia," Whit presses. "Prove it!"

"Okay, Whitford. I can do that. Tell me, does this line sound familiar? *'We only have a short time together. Let's not waste it.'*"

Judging from the shade of gray my brother turns, he *has* heard those particular words before.

"Had a dream the other day, didn't you? And Celia wore a lot of perfume, right?"

I've seen fireplace ashes with more flesh color than Whit has right now.

"And you know *why* she was wearing so much perfume? It's because even in a dream, *she stinks like a rotting zombie* — the way all Lost Ones stink."

Whit is shaking his head in denial, or disgust, or horror. Or all of the above.

"But you know the irony here? She's not haunting you because she loves you. Or because she wants you back. No, she's after somebody else."

"What do you mean?" Whit asks.

"In fact, the deal she struck with me — the reason I was allowed to live and return here — was that she made me promise to bring her *your sister.* That's what this is all about, jockstrap."

Chapter 92

Whit

I CAN'T EVEN BEGIN to understand what Byron Swain just told me. It has to be lies.

I have a plan forming, but in the meantime, I pick up every object within grabbing range and start hurling it out the window at him and his beasts. Books, candlesticks, cook's tools, framed pictures. You name it, I toss it outside.

I have a good throwing arm, but unfortunately the little creep is obviously experienced at dodging projectiles.

"Wisty!" he shouts in between ducks. "*Please* come with me! This is your last chance to accept my offer. Do what your parents have been preparing you for your whole life!"

At that, I hurl a standing lamp at him like a spear. It hits Byron in the side and spins him around, but he doesn't go down.

Then Wisty stuns me. In the quietest voice, she whispers, "Mom and Dad *did* say... that sometimes we needed to do things that won't feel natural."

"They said 'outside of your comfort zone,' not *stupid!*" I yell at Wisty. Immediately I regret it. But it's too late. Even Byron rises out of his defensive crouch and glares at me.

"Did you just call your sister stupid, Whit?" he shouts.

"No." In a sense. "I told her going anywhere with *you* was stupid. And it is."

"Well, you've denigrated Wisty for the last time."

"Byron!" Wisty calls urgently. "It's fine! I swear! It's an affectionate nickname!"

"Sayonara, Whitford Allgood," Byron says, and throws me a rigid salute.

And that's when he blows a new tune on his Command Pipe, and the Kill Team reengages in the hunt—by climbing ape-style up the side of the building and crashing through what's left of the windows.

Well, I guess we thought coming here to Mrs. Highsmith's would be a game changer. Looks like it is.

Chapter 93

Wisty

I AM NOT MUCH OF A COWARDLY screamer by nature, but two tons of growling, pouncing ape-kids swarming into a tiny apartment with one barricaded exit definitely elicits a shriek from me that is totally *bloodcurdling*.

It actually startles the Kill Team for a split second, long enough for a pause in which Byron pipes another series of commands up at them.

Whit fairly hurls me into a corner of the room, then blocks the path to me with his body.

"Whit, *that isn't going to work!*"

And it sure doesn't. The fiends practically run over my poor brother, shouting in murderous glee. But they don't kill us. They hog-tie Whit and me, quickly, viciously.

And then in walks Byron Swain.

"Sorry about all the safety precautions, Wisty," says Byron. He checks the ropes on our arms and forces a gag into Whit's mouth. "But I can't have any more distractions while I make good on my commitment here. In case you think I'm not a decent fellow," he says as he turns and forces an oily-tasting rag into my mouth, too, "I should point out that I'm not going to have my friends here tear Whit apart in front of you, as instructed. Instead, I'll have both of you sent along to The One. I'm guessing he'll probably want to put you on the same weight-loss program as your parents. Then, as promised, on to the Allgood execution!"

He didn't really say that just now. There's no freaking way he really—

"Yes, sir. That's going to be one majorly popular execution-palooza." He goes right on talking. "I warned you, Wisty. I tried to stop this."

Okay, Byron, I think to myself. *This is real simple. You leave me no choice. I'm just going to…EXPLODE.*

Chapter 94

Whit

WHEN MY LITTLE SISTER FLARES up in anger, sometimes she's just a regular, run-of-the-mill human torch with fire swirling all around her body, and you would definitely be well-advised not to shake her hand. Other times, though, she's so bright and hot, it's hard even to *look* at her. Like right now.

But Byron *does* look at her. In fact, he's totally gaga, like he's never been so impressed with her skills.

Wisty's ropes and gag last all of a nanosecond as she bounds up from the ground and takes a couple of menacing swipes at Byron's freaky death squad. They wisely move back a few stuttering steps. I'm certain she could smoke their wiry butts into ash, but for some reason she doesn't.

While the ape-kids recoil, Byron steps closer to Wisty. He looks to be in a daze. He absently drops his Command Pipe as his eyes glaze over.

Wisty waves her hands wildly. "Get away from me, Byron! I'm as hot as a hundred furnaces. Just leave now and I won't hurt you!"

"You *can't* hurt me, Wisty," he says. "Not anymore." Then he does the unthinkable. I'm bound and gagged and can't do a thing as I watch Byron throw himself right into Wisty's flames. She tries to pull away, but then he's clutching her as if he's a child and she's here to rescue him.

Wisty was right. We're not murderers. As much as I hate this kid, I can't sit still and let Byron immolate himself.

"Byron! What're you *doing? Stop!*" Wisty yells. "Stop, drop, and roll!"

"You can't hurt me, Wisty," Byron repeats dreamily, despite the crackling and hissing flame surrounding him. He must be delirious. Obviously he's being burned to death, but he's showing absolutely no signs of pain.

The feral kids, confused and without any command to guide them, are starting to growl again. But Byron is oblivious, his face buried in Wisty's neck, his arms wrapped around her. As if he's drinking in her fire.

And... he's not burning.

He's not burning!

Chapter 95

Whit

TO REVIEW: THERE ARE any number of life-threatening crises on our hands at the moment.

1) Byron's gone loco.
2) In a few minutes his wild, feral team may go from chilling to *killing*.
3) Mrs. H.'s apartment is a major fire hazard, and Wisty's humongous flames have already lit up all the curtains, the rug, and the wallpaper, which is badly burned.
4) I'm still at risk of being hauled off to The One if I can't get control of the situation.

I have to try to extinguish Wisty's flames somehow. But I can't control fire. I know it in my bones — that's Wisty's Gift. But if I focus on Mrs. H.'s cauldron — *Can I move it?* It's filled with liquid, after all.

The pack is growling louder and louder, so I have no choice.

It's an act of desperation, but I focus my mind and manage to lift Mrs. Highsmith's barrel. Then I *will* it to fly across the room.

Whatever Mrs. H. was cooking, I'm not sure it was fit for human consumption, since it's as effective as foam from a fire extinguisher. Wisty's flame flickers out, and Byron — with no trace of burnt clothing, hair, or skin — drops to the floor.

Wisty's dripping with gruel and rather dazed by what just happened but still sharp enough to realize what she should do next. She unbinds me and removes my gag, all the while staring at the ape-kids, who definitely seem to respect her abilities with fire.

"You stay back or I'll fry you!" she warns. She even throws off a few fresh, sizzling flames.

Then my little sister helps me up, and I realize she's a lot stronger than she looks. "That was so totally messed up," she says quietly. "Let's get out of here while we still can."

Chapter 96

Wisty

AS TOTALLY SCREWED UP as the past hour was—from my mom and dad's deeply disturbing message, to battling hurricane gales, to the utterly unforgettable experience of Byron Swain embracing, absorbing, *breathing* in my fire—I still leave the building feeling inexplicably powerful. I'm learning something about myself, even though it's not clear what it is and why The One wants it so badly.

As soon as Whit and I get outside Mrs. H.'s building, there's an incredible windstorm, which can only mean One thing. And you know what? I'm not even that surprised anymore. He is, I hate to say, *omnipresent*.

I whirl around to face him, as if this is a gunfight. The One is slowly walking up the abandoned street toward us. "This is the grand finale, children of Allgood!" he calls out in warning, which seems unusually fair of him.

"I've given that wretched informant more than enough chances," he continues as he calmly marches forward. "I said that if he failed in his mission, he would be made to suffer—by watching you die slowly and painfully by my hand.

"But since I'm nothing if not evenhanded, one *final test*. This will be a *pass-fail* for you and your brother. Maybe the two of you survive, maybe one, probably none. Are you ready, children?" He doesn't wait for an answer. "Then *let us begin!*"

He stomps the ground with his foot, and an enormous crevasse opens wide and starts racing down the middle of the street, headed right for us.

"I control the earth!" he yells at the top of his lungs. "True or false?"

Whit takes my hand and squeezes. It's amazing how much a little human touch can do. It gives me the boost I need. "We could fly?" I say.

"Worth a try. Focus, now. We can do this."

It's about the fastest morph I've ever done—double-morph, to be exact—and in an instant Whit and I are aloft. Becoming hawks requires a lot more energy than changing into hummingbirds, but I'm filled with a charge and I really let loose. The rush is amazing. Usually The One's very presence is magic-crushing, but right now I feel we're unbeatable as we start pumping our wings triumphantly above the city.

But it's only for about two hundred yards—until a wall of wind hits. We try to catch it and ride it, but the sheer power and force send us careening sideways and then downward.

"I control the wind, the air!" The One bellows. "True or false?"

Whit and I are nearly thrown into one side of a brick-faced office building. But before I have a chance to panic, I've managed to turn us into the first animal I can think of with protective armor: an armadillo. Two of them. We curl up into armored balls and safely bounce off the wall—which, by the way, still hurts—and then we roll down onto the street.

But another huge chasm opens in front of us, accompanied by the roar of the angry One.

"I control the cities and the streets. True or false? I'll give you a hint—*that statement is true.*"

The roadway suddenly explodes into shafts of rock metamorphosing instantly into shimmering crystal, sending razor-sharp shrapnel in all directions. If Whit and I aren't off the ground in a second, we're going to be sliced into nothing.

We leap harder and higher, until I feel not only wings but paws. We're part lion, part bird... the legendary griffin of folklore.

We can transform ourselves into the stuff of imagination?

There are no words for that mind-boggling realization. But it's forgotten in an instant when the spot where we'd just been explodes with a thundering crack. The two buildings on either side of the street collapse. A shock wave and a blast of dust rise after us and send us spinning.

It's dizzying to body and mind. Our power is pretty good, but his is unbelievably over-whelming. *Why is he so powerful? Who could control nature like this?*

I have a terrible, terrible thought.

Maybe he's God?

There he is. So much larger than life, arms outstretched, eyes locked on us, dark suit impeccable. His mouth works furiously as he summons what appears to be a typhoon out of the sky, spinning toward us.

The herculean-force wind and rain pum-meling our wings is too much for them to bear, and we plunge toward the water of the harbor below.

"Extra-credit question!" screams The One. "Who controls the water, the oceans, the riv-ers, the seas? Oops, time's up. Pens down. *I do!*"

Chapter 97

Whit

I GUESS WE FAILED his test. But we won't surrender, no way. That isn't going to happen.

The force of hitting the water might have knocked us out and drowned us if Wisty and I hadn't been almost perfectly in sync. We pull off a near splashless dive and slice through the surface. But underneath, the water is churning and rushing up from the bottom of the sea.

Who controls the water? Who else?

The entire harbor is piling up into one enormous wave—a tsunami to end all tsunamis—and we're floundering, swimming right in the middle of it. Higher and higher it builds. I've never seen anything like it. I think it's safe to assume no one has. Unless we're supposed to take the Great Book literally. *Are we?*

Wisty and I can't force our way downward against the surge. It's useless even trying to swim at this point. *If you can't beat it, join it, right?*

And so I imagine us...*on longboards.* And it actually happens!

"*You* did that?" Wisty yells as she steadies her footing on the surfboard.

"Yeah!" I shout. "Even if we crash and drown, it'll be some kind of a ride!"

Wisty smiles a crazed surfer-girl grin at me as the wave starts to go down—as *we* start to go down.

Chapter 98

Wisty

IN ABOUT ONE AND a half seconds, my very brief euphoria changes to dread. Suddenly this massive wave is gaining height again. We're approaching shore and we're maybe a quarter mile in the air. The One's going to wipe out a major chunk of the city if he doesn't stop this madness right now. And that means there are hundreds — make that thousands — of people in terrible danger of being drowned.

Even though I figure that many of them are New Order automatons, I keep telling myself they're living, breathing human beings. And we can't let this giant wave — or The One — crush them. I think I know what I have to do, and there's no time to consult with Whit.

It's what my parents were saying: sometimes for the good of the many, you have to do something way outside your comfort zone. And this, dear reader, is *way* outside what I would consider even borderline sanity.

Over the roar of the massive wave, I yell so loudly I think the force of the words is going to tear my throat open. *"I'll give you what you want! I'll give you my Gift! Just stop this insanity before the wave hits shore!"*

Like magic—or maybe I should say it *was* magic—the wave starts to lower and then we're gently coasting toward a narrow shoreline of packed sand.

Standing there is none other than The One. He's smiling like a proud dad welcoming his kids home from a long trip.

"What an amazing ride! Ah, to be young... I envy you!" he says as the wave calmly spreads itself across the shore and we drift to a stop.

"I'm so pleased you've come to your senses, Wisty," says The One. Unfortunately, I have rather sad news. You fail—both of you. All of the Allgoods fail. It's obvious that I can't work with you, so I suppose...I have to work without you."

He turns so his back is facing us and raises his hands to the heavens.

"Take them away!" he bellows. "I have no further use for this witch and wizard."

But there's no one there. *He's talking to no one.*

And then, in a heartbeat, like a plague of locusts overtaking the land, thousands of New Order soldiers and police swarm over the crest of the hill and descend upon us.

We swirl around, only to be confronted by even more hordes of soldiers standing in the water.

This wall of evil is impenetrable.

Finally The One looks back at us. "There is a moral to this story," he says. "Of those who receive Gifts, much is expected. Take that one to the Shadowland with you, witch and wizard."

EPILOGUE

AS PROMISED, A SPECTACLE

Chapter 99

Wisty

I KNOW THERE'S NOT many pages left in this book, so at this point you're wondering where the happy ending is.

I may be pretty young, but I've figured out that life doesn't get wrapped up into neat little endings with perfect little bows. I can promise you one thing, though: there's hope, okay? Don't ever call me, Wisteria Rose Allgood, a *downer*. No matter what crap The One shovels upon us, I swear I'll find that single bright spot in the bitterly dark landscape and cling to it for dear life.

And right now I'm clinging to the sight of the very people who gave *me* dear life.

My mother and father!

Not ghosts, not hallucinations, but live and in the flesh. But in ropes. Just like me. At least Whit and I can see them and tell them how much we love them—one last time before we die.

But what a family reunion it's turning out to be! Look at us here—the jeering crowd around us, the jackbooted New Order lackeys shoving us forward onto the stadium stage, the ropes around our necks, the TV cameras in our faces...and, in the tower, right in front of us, *Him*. The One Who Is The One. He's in his glory, triumphant—he's won!

Using the old hangman's platform as his stage just digs the knife in. Vaporization is The One's preferred method of execution—it's highly efficient—but the nooses are a bonus in our extra-cruel humiliation, the morbid theater of it all.

I *so* want to burn up with hatred for this monster who has destroyed our life and is about to kill my entire family. I want to use my anger to find my strength, to find my magic, to burn this horrible scene to ashes, to cauterize this place right off the face of this so-called world.

But honestly I'm too terrified to be angry. My courage is crumbling; my light is fading.

Oh God, I don't want to die right now. I don't want my family to die. I don't want to watch them die.

Dad's still wearing his game face, trying to give me and Whit courage. Mom's given up attempting to hide her emotions and is quietly crying in grief and fear.

Whit, on the other hand, looks wildly angry, at least when he's not recovering from repeated blows to the back of his head. Half a dozen times now he's surged against his bonds, and half a dozen times his hooded handlers have struck him with a billy club, sending him limply to his knees until they haul him back up and he tries to find the focus and strength to surge again.

The ghoulish crowd is loving every dramatic bit of this. The heartbroken mother, the stoic father, the defiant son, the quaking chicken-liver daughter who they have somehow come to believe is a powerful witch.

But now The One Who Is The One raises his long-fingered hands in the air and waves for them to be quiet.

And now he's doing something else with his hands, a motion I know only too well. *Oh God, please don't let him—*

A black rift opens in front of him and rips its way toward us. Or, at least, *toward two of us.*

And, just like that, Mom and Dad have been vaporized. There's nothing left but smoke. My mother. My father. Gone.

Chapter 100

Wisty

WHIT AND I STARE in paralyzed horror as a wisp of black ash lifts in the breeze and moves out across the sea of onlookers. They're stomping, fist-pumping, and roaring their approval of the disgraceful murders that just took place.

I'm too decimated by the grief and shock of it to take any joy in the fact that we are—inexplicably—still alive. The One didn't kill us. *He didn't kill us.* It makes no sense.

And then it gets even stranger, even more surreal. Like a dream.

The scene is suddenly awash with painfully blinding light. But it's a chilling light, if there is such a thing, like a powerful tsunami of sun blasting over a landscape of ice.

Maybe I'm dead after all? Maybe this is that celebrated light at the end of the tunnel?

Or... is it the End of Days?

When the light ebbs, I see that The One Who Is The One is on his knees. *Screaming.* Only for some reason I can't hear him. In fact, I can't hear anything.

Was there an explosion? I don't know, but suddenly there are hands all over me, cold hands. They're loosening my ropes. A small army of hooded figures has banded around me and Whit. The New Order guards lining the stage have been toppled by the rush of flooding light and energy.

No sooner have the hooded figures pulled the nooses up over our heads than the hangman's trapdoors on which we've been standing click open. And I'm falling into darkness.

It's as if I've been hanged, but I haven't been, have I? I've just fallen onto my back.

I'm sprawled on the ground with all the spirit and decorum of a discarded rag doll. I don't care to move. I don't even care to breathe. I just want this all to end. I want to close my eyes and stop *being.* I pray for it to happen.

There's another cold hand on my arm, helping me to my feet. And now my ears are starting to ring, and I hear something else, too—a voice. A familiar voice.

"Run," the voice says as a door opens and daylight streams in. "Run, Wisteria. Run like there's no tomorrow...because if you don't, maybe there won't be."

My hearing returns as the sound of massive panic sweeping through the stands hits me. The shrieks and wails seem to have enough power to bring down the entire stadium.

What have they seen? *What has happened to their fearless leader?*

I stagger outside and join the frantic crowd on the stadium field streaming toward one of the four tunnel exits. I have done this before: escape the scene of my own execution. It seems impossible, but I know I can do this. I know how to keep my head down. I know how to duck and weave. I know how to stay focused in a sea of blind panic.

But I haven't gone fifty yards when I stop dead, as if my heart has fallen from my chest. *Whit! Where is Whit?*

I turn and manage to glimpse the plywood hangman's scaffold. Four empty nooses dangle limply in the breeze. The One is nowhere to be seen.

Neither is Whit.

I haven't even cried for my parents yet, but now I fall to my knees and start to bawl like a baby. In an ocean of thousands, I'm alone.

But not completely. Again there's a hand on my arm and a voice in my ear. "Run, Wisteria," it says. "Hurry. You have to leave this cursed place."

But this time I resist. I get to my feet, but I'm pushing back toward the scaffold, toward the last place I saw my brother.

I make it only a few steps when somebody — or something — knocks me to the ground.

"Whitford's fine," it says, pulling me back to my feet and turning me around. "*Think* about it. You can't be together now. It would make it easier on them if you were together. We can't risk it."

The voice has been rational, if insistent. But now it sounds truly urgent. "There's no time, Wisty. For Whit's sake, run! Run. You have

The Gift. Only you have it. Without you, hope will die."

And I have to run, don't I? I have to try to escape. My life matters. My Gift matters. So I run. I run as if my brother's life depends on it.

As I look back, I finally see the face of the one who rescued me — it's Celia. *Celia!*

There she is — that one bright spot in the bitterly dark landscape. I told you I would find it. I told you I would cling to that light for dear life. And I am.

I'll use it to find Whit. To find my friends. And to make my way to the Shadowland to find my parents.

Because...

Of bad, scary witches who are given Great Gifts, Much Is Expected.

TO BE CONTINUED

Excerpts of
NEW ORDER
PROPAGANDA

as Disseminated by
The Council of N.O. "Arts"

ESPECIALLY OFFENSIVE BOOKS THAT HAVE BEEN BANNED

as Dictated by The One Who Bans Books

THE BRAWLERS: The story of a pack of sentient dogs—some stray, some pets—seeking to fulfill a "prophecy." Thankfully, since New Order citizens are now aware that pet ownership is irrational and a burden on society (and that the only appropriate role for canine beasts is in the employ of members of the Hunt), there is little interest in this series.

GOSSIP GHOST: A series of books that follows a roaming pack of teenage spirits who lie, cheat, and spy on one another. According to the New Order Council for Documenting Pernicious Influences, the lying, cheating, and spying were reasonably well done, but the supernatural elements were offensive. The books were among the first to be rounded up and destroyed in the Great Book Purge.

THE INTERESTING CROSSOVER OF THE DOG TO THE SHADOWLAND: The purportedly nonfiction story of a dog, more exploratory than the rest of his pack, crossing into another dimension. Because of nonsensical references to alternate dimensions, the text was banned.

THE THIRST TOURNAMENT: A work of fiction set in a world that has run out of water and where the government has decided to control the population by having excess children serve as gladiators. After a thorough investigation, the New Order Council on Resource Protection has declared this to be an unrealistic water-rationing strategy.

THE UNFORTUNATE STONES: In this absurd novel, a group of actors are turned into stones in a publicity stunt gone horribly wrong. They spend the majority of the book contemplating their stony bodies and the afterlife. References to the dark arts, theatrics, and the afterlife quickly earned the novel an Objectionable Mention on the New Order Book

Burning Committee's list of tomes to be destroyed.

ULTIMATE ARMSTRONG: The absurd tales of a collective of genetically altered children with wings who can fly. As The One Who Is The One once quipped, these books should be read just as soon as pigs fly.

SOME PARTICULARLY REPREHENSIBLE NOISE POLLUTERS OF THE FORMER AGE

as Defined by The One Who Monitors Auditory Stimuli

DUCHESS GOO GOO: A ridiculous pop star who burst on the scene with her dangerously infectious first single, "Five-Card Stud." She dominated the charts of the day and used her theatrical wiles to beguile the mass media into abetting her celebrity ambitions. She was among the first musical celebrities rounded up by the New Order Council of Cultural Standards.

DUSTIN BEEPER: A singer propelled into stardom by the videos posted online from his debut album, *Beepin' & Weepin'*, which spread like a viral pandemic. Though officially banned for entertainment purposes, his music is still sometimes used by the New Order to lure Freelanders out of hiding.

THE RED-EYED SLEAZES: A "hip-hop" group whose disturbing videos proudly projected tacky excess and bikini-clad girls, and yet the musicians always seemed as if they'd just like to go to sleep. The New Order Council of Musical Standards had them banned for their oblique mockery of N.O. professional culture.

SMILEY PYRUS: A teenage pop star who rose to stardom by deceitfully charming her audience with a shy smile and then literally setting the music charts on fire. While not as dangerous as the wanted witch Wisteria Allgood, Smiley still is among the most dangerous musical fugitives in Freeland.

SWIFTY TAILOR: Country music superstar who was as famous for her bouncing blond curls and silly romantic folk songs as she was for breaking the hearts of handsome movie stars. Upon the arrival of Order to the world, she was *swiftly* jailed for her insistence on referencing "romance" and "love" in her work.

VISUAL "ARTISTS" WHO ARE NO LONGER SULLYING THE WORLD

as Annotated by The One Who Assesses Visual Stimuli

PIERRE PONDRIAN: While briefly embraced by the N.O. as a representative of efficiency, this minimalist was soon banned when it was discovered his work resonated with anti-establishment forces glorifying the virtues of "abstraction" and "freethinking."

PAULO CEZONNE: A lazy painter who was involved with the "impressionist" movement, which the New Order deemed damaging to the development of clear and precise thinking. The movement proved as tremendously difficult to stamp out as an antibiotic-resistant infectious disease.

RANCHER ELFIE: A misguided "pop culture" artist who thought it would be amusing to mock the New Order by emulating official statements, posters, and banners and replacing certain messages and icons with absurd substitutions of his own design. He and his sense of humor are no longer with us.

SANDY EYEHOLE: A photographer who covered his prints of various celebrities and "commercial" artifacts with garishly colored sand. Fortunately his work was very easy to destroy.

SEPTEMBRE FEYNOIR: This artist's saccharine depictions of pretty children, gowned women, bucolic landscapes, and domestic scenes—cheap prints of which were once embraced and consumed by millions—are now regarded as bad for one's health, with some studies indicating they may be carcinogenic.

THANKSY: An oddly polite purveyor of graffiti who, during the last battle before the New Order's Great Ascendancy, painted "Thanks!" over doorways that were hospitable to his rebel propaganda. Later, the markings proved useful to New Order agents looking to eliminate subversive elements.

EGREGIOUSLY INEFFICIENT OR SUBVERSIVE WORDS BANNED FROM USE

by Decree of The One Who Edits the Dictionary

Beaner (noun)
a derogatory term for people who have the good sense to pay attention to the important things in everyday life, such as budgets, performance reviews, and municipal statistics *<usage instance:* As she stood on the execution platform, the rebel screamed her defiance at the noble citizenry, calling the spectators a pack of *Beaners.>*

pilgarlic (noun)
an archaic construct formerly used to describe a man without a full head of hair *<usage instance:* It was ironic that the swordsman mocked his bald-headed foe as a *pilgarlic,* for in a few hundred years baldness would become the height of personal attractiveness.>

sandwich (noun)
an archaic term for two slices of bread placed

around some sort of foodstuff—because of the unfortunate phonetic properties of the latter half of this word, The One Who Is The One lent his revered name to the lexicon, and this item is now referred to as a One-der-Meal <*usage instance:* Anybody calling a One-der-Meal a *sandwich* will soon find himself accustomed to prison rations.>

shademark (noun)
a silly word rebels use to scare their children— it apparently refers to the stain on the ground left by a person who has fallen prey to a "Lost One," a zombielike creature that inhabits their fantastical realm of spirits <*usage instance:* Terrified by stories of *shademarks,* the child had sleep-depriving nightmares that seriously impinged upon his productivity at the factory.>

wisteria (noun)
a climbing ornamental vine with fragrant, usually purple, clusters of flowers—for obvious reasons, mention of this now extinct species of plant is prohibited <*usage instance:* The

gardener tore out the ugly stump of *wisteria* and in its place planted a New Order Soybean Cultivar No. A42.>

wunny (adjective)
an unpleasant expression apparently used by rebels to describe any unpleasant situation (etymology uncertain) *<usage instance:* Dude, this Resistance rally is totally *wunny.* Let's get out of here.>

About the Authors

JAMES PATTERSON is the internationally bestselling author of the highly praised Maximum Ride novels, the Witch & Wizard series, the Daniel X series, *Med Head,* and the detective series featuring Alex Cross and the Women's Murder Club. His books have sold more than 205 million copies worldwide, making him one of the bestselling authors of all time. He lives in Florida.

For previews of forthcoming James Patterson books and more information about the author, go to www.JamesPatterson.com.

NED RUST lives in Croton, New York, with his family. He has also collaborated with James Patterson on *Daniel X: Watch the Skies.*

HULK 3/2022